109

D1095629

E X   L I B R I S

MELISSA ANN CLARKE

The Mystery of
Lonesome Manor

Other books by the author:

THE MYSTERY OF THE CREAKING WINDMILL
THE SECRET OF THE SINGING TOWER
BIG INDIAN AND LITTLE BEAR
THE SECRET OF THE OLD COACH INN
THE PAPOOSE WHO WOULDN'T KEEP HER
    STOCKINGS ON
YOU CAN'T KEEP A SQUIRREL ON THE GROUND

The Mystery of Lonesome Manor

by HARRIET EVATT

Illustrated by DAVID STONE

THE **BOBBS-MERRILL** COMPANY, INC.
A SUBSIDIARY OF HOWARD W. SAMS & CO., INC.
Publishers · INDIANAPOLIS · NEW YORK

Copyright © 1962 by The Bobbs-Merrill Company, Inc.
Printed in the United States of America
Library of Congress Catalog Card Number: 62-11980
First Printing

To my husband
William S. Evatt

Contents

The Mystery of
Lonesome Manor

CHAPTER 1

A Gift from a Stranger

THE CHEERFUL sound of the single bell worn on the harness of a large brown farm horse filled the wintry dusk with the melody heard throughout the farm country of French Canada when it lies beneath a mantle of snow.

The horse was drawing a heavy sledge along the winding road that encircled the Island of Orléans like a white ribbon.

Perched on the high wooden seat of the sledge, her knees under a bearskin robe, sat Alouette Robinette, driving her father's horse, Herbert, with the hands of an expert.

"Whoa, Herbert!" She drew the big sledge to the side of the road, the red pompon atop her woolen cap nodding in the cold wind that blew across the St. Lawrence River.

"It is the butcher," Alouette said to herself, peering through the snow as the sleigh came abreast of her.

" 'Allo, Featherhead," the butcher called, waving a mittened hand in cheery greeting.

Alouette returned his greeting as cordially as it was extended, but after the butcher was out of earshot she very distinctly said, "Pooh!"

She said it so wholeheartedly that Herbert looked over his shoulder in surprise.

"Oh, it's not that I don't like the butcher," she sputtered. "But, my goodness, why do I always have to be reminded of that silly song, 'Alouette, Alouette'? Because the Alouette in the song was a featherhead, they call me by such a foolish nickname. Featherhead indeed!"

She gave the old farm horse free rein now, and he set off briskly toward the Robinette farmhouse and the comfortable old barn, where good sweet oats waited for him.

Lights were twinkling from all the farmhouse windows, throwing orange-colored squares on the snow as the dark blue dusk set in. *Clop, clop, clop.* The soft sound of Herbert's hoofs in the snow was accompanied by the jolting bumps of the farm sledge. The sledge was so bumpy that it was difficult for Alouette to maintain her high perch on the backless wooden seat.

"My goodness, Herbert! This road is like a washboard," she complained. "Slow down a little, please."

But Herbert was in no mood for slowing down, with supper and the warm barn so close at hand. So Alouette Robinette, who loved horses and knew how to handle them better than any girl on the Island of Orléans, stopped complaining. She started whistling as she always did when driving down the long road toward home.

Now the white road curved, and the little farm girl with the taffy-colored braids beneath her red woolen hood came into view of the deserted old house called Lonesome Manor.

The old Manor had many turrets and towers. It stood dark and frowning behind an avenue of tall, pointing trees, and appeared to be guarding some strange secret behind its gray stone wall and locked iron gates.

Many, many years ago, Lonesome Manor had been built by a Scottish officer, the first Laird, who had been presented with the land by General Wolfe himself as a reward for bravery and services to the Crown.

Alouette drew in the reins and sat staring up at the dismal house. A small chill plucked at her spine, and she no longer whistled.

All the surrounding farmhouses were twinkling with cheerful lights. From their warm kitchens came the tempting and delicious smells of the farmwives' excellent cooking.

But there were no lights in the old Manor, no cheerful smells of supper under way . . . only darkness and bitter cold as the wind blew in from the river.

"It does look scary, Herbert, but Grandmère says all the stories they tell about the house are only silly tales thought up by foolish gossips in chimney corners."

And now, as she watched, the old house seemed to recede into the distance behind the silently falling snow. True or not, the stories had been repeated throughout the years, and had even grown in the retelling.

A treasure, it was whispered, was hidden somewhere within the Manor walls, placed there by the first Laird, who had been carried off by savage Indians and had never returned.

It was thought that the Laird's Treasure (as it was called) might be hidden in one of the round towers atop the building; probably in the one tower that had no windows. What was the mystery about this windowless tower? Was there a stairway leading to it? If this was so, no one had ever found it. The old Manor had guarded its secret well, if the legends about it were were true.

Another tower had a widow's walk. Why? Grandmother Robinette had explained this to Alouette in a very logical manner. There was nothing unusual in the old house's having a walk or railing around one of its towers. The Laird could mount the ladder from the floor beneath and overlook his fine farmland. He could also watch for marauding bands of Indians that were a constant threat to the island in those early days.

"Poor old Lonesome Manor," Alouette thought. "It looks so unhappy, standing there, deserted, in the snow.

"Oh, the snow is coming down faster! Giddap, Herbert," she called. The big farm horse set off at a lively clip, and Alouette began to whistle again in the cold winter air.

In one of the farmhouses Alouette had to pass lived Madame Durand, the village gossip. Ma-

15

dame Durand did not approve of whistling or any sign of joy in living.

Now, as the old sledge with the small figure perched atop its wooden seat went jolting by, Madame Durand pulled her curtain aside and peered through her snowy window.

"Do you hear what I hear?" she asked her husband, who was dozing in the chimney corner. "That Alouette Robinette is bouncing down the road in that old sledge, whistling again. 'Featherhead!' An excellent name for her, and for all the Robinettes. They are all a bunch of featherheads, laughing and whistling and never seeming to have a care in the world. All featherheads, if you ask me."

"No one did ask you," her husband muttered sleepily.

"All those children, six of them mind you, all those mouths to feed." Madame's chief joy was thrusting her sharp nose into other people's affairs.

"Look at the way their cousin, Jacques Robinette, ran away. And there she goes, whistling as if nothing had ever happened. 'A whistling girl and a crowing hen always come to some bad end,' " she quoted.

16

"What happened to their cousin, Jacques Robinette, happened when Alouette was very young—as young as her little sister Chichi who, I believe, is now approaching the ripe old age of five," said Monsieur Durand crossly.

Madame let the curtain fall and confronted her spouse. "Whistling as her cousin Jacques used to whistle, going down this very road! Humph!"

Monsieur Durand made a religious sign. "I would not speak ill of those who have passed to the beyond," he said sternly. "He was whistling to let the girl he loved know he was on his way to see her. I recall when the banns were published and later when the town crier came out on the steps of the church and announced the betrothal after services. And now, the two of them are gone, gone forever."

But there was no stopping Madame Durand.

"That Alouette, whistling out there, even up to the very gate of Lonesome Manor, when other children are afraid even to pass it at dusk!"

The starched frill on Madame's cap rustled with her pious indignation. "I tell you, life is a serious thing. It is wicked to take it so lightly."

But a deep snore was her only response. Her good husband had covered his face with a large red handkerchief and gone peacefully, if noisily, back to sleep.

Meanwhile, Alouette, unaware that she was being watched and discussed by the village gossip, rode happily down the road, whistling in tune with the brass bell on Herbert's harness.

But as she neared the gate to the lane that led to the Robinette farmhouse, a figure seemed to appear from nowhere out of the snowstorm, and to loom up beside the sledge.

"How!" A man was standing with right hand held high in an Indian's peaceful greeting.

"How . . . how!" quavered Alouette. "I . . . I didn't see you coming, it's snowing so hard."

Alouette brushed the snow from her eyes and peered at the stranger. She thought, "It *is* an Indian, and he is on snowshoes."

The man stood and waited as Alouette looked at him. His long black hair was partially covered by a wide-brimmed hat with a round crown. His clothing was made of deerskin.

She knew all the friendly Hurons who came from the Indian village of Lorette by sight, but this man was a stranger.

At last the Indian spoke: "Where you think you go so fast?"

"I don't think, I *know*. I'm going home to supper."

"Nice warm supper, eh?"

"Of course. Doesn't everyone go home to a warm supper in the wintertime?"

"Not all. Some wander on face of earth. Sometimes warm supper, sometimes no.

"You live near?" he asked suddenly, changing the subject.

"Yes, up there." Alouette pointed toward the lane.

Herbert moved restlessly and pawed the snow. It was his suppertime, too, and he was growing impatient. Still the stranger seemed reluctant to let her go.

Alouette began to be frightened. "Look here," she said. "If you are hungry and will follow me up the lane to the house, Maman and Grandmère will give you supper. No one has ever left the Robinette kitchen hungry."

"Ahha . . . that *is* Robinette farm!" the man said, ignoring her invitation.

"Certainly. Everyone knows that."

"No. You be Alouette Robinette? And is Christmas tree grove back your house?"

Alouette nodded. "Yes, I am Alouette, and

Grandpère raises Christmas trees to sell in Quebec at the Christmas market."

"You are called Little Featherhead."

"Yes. Who knows that better than I do?"

"This your birthday but one sun. Tomorrow, you be eleven years. Is true?"

"Yes."

"What you think this?" The stranger reached into his pocket and dangled something before her startled eyes.

"Oh, what a beautiful ring!" The Indian was holding up a ring on a golden chain . . . a ring unlike anything she had ever seen. Set in a wreath of flashing green stones was a milky gray stone. As she looked at it closely she discovered that a light streak ran through the center of the stone, for all the world like the pupil in the eye of a cat.

"Why it is beautiful . . . it . . . it looks like a cat's eye!" she gasped.

"That name of stone. It cat's eye, and emeralds around," the Indian said, placing it in the palm of her hand. "This rare and old ring. Is but one other . . ." He broke off, then said, "It is for you, the ring, if you do two things."

Alouette nodded, her fascinated eyes held by some mystic spell the beautiful ring seemed to work on her.

"First thing is you tell no one about ring, not show to any, not even family," the man explained.

"I promise. And what then?"

"You know tune 'Alouette'? If yes, whistle for me."

"Oh, yes. My uncle, Jacques Robinette, taught me to whistle that tune." And once again Alouette's clear, birdlike whistle broke the winter silence.

21

The Indian nodded. "Now whistle 'Frère Jacques.'"

Alouette did as he asked her.

"Why are you asking me to whistle these old French songs?"

"Because Alouette and Jacques belong together," was the mysterious answer.

"Now here keepsake for you from way-off Manitoba," he said, "because I know you one I seek." And he closed the fingers of her mittened hand over the beautiful ring on its golden chain.

"But who are you then?"

"Call me Northern Traveler."

Alouette looked up then and said, "Thank you. Oh, thank you! The ring is so beautiful. Thank you, Northern Traveler."

But there was no one there to hear her. The stranger had disappeared as silently as he had come, vanishing into the snowstorm. Even the tracks of his snowshoes were disappearing. There was nothing to do but slip the ring and the chain into her pocket. She turned Herbert up the lane toward the warm barn and the twinkling lights of the friendly old farmhouse.

It was growing bitterly cold as the wind blew in from the St. Lawrence River, but Alouette did not notice the cold. She was turning the Northern Traveler's words over and over in her mind. "A keepsake for you, from way-off Manitoba," the stranger had said.

"But who, then?"

The little farm girl, born on the Island of Orléans, did not know a living soul in faraway Manitoba.

CHAPTER 2

A Mysterious Word

"WHERE in this world have you been, Featherhead?" A figure emerged from the dark interior of the barn.

It was her brother André, one year younger than Alouette, who was the eldest of the Robinette brood of six.

"Pooh!" Alouette tossed her head and her pigtails bristled beneath her woolen cap as they did when anyone called her Featherhead.

"Oh come on, Alouette. I was only teasing you. I'll unharness Herbert and feed him for you. It's almost your birthday," her brother said. "I'm sorry I called you Featherhead."

"Well then, I'll forgive you," said Alouette, and

made her way to the side door. Here she vigorously swept the snow from her boots with the broom that always hung beside the kitchen-parlor door in winter.

"Oh, what a heavenly smell," she cried as she opened the door.

"It's split pea soup with ham tonight, *chérie*," said her mother, "but tomorrow is your birthday . . . and there will be a feast."

"Then you will see a cake this big around," piped the fair-haired, five-year-old Chichi, making a large circle with her arms. "The biggest cake in the world, I bet."

"I'll bet," Alouette agreed.

"You brought me something from the store, Alouette? You didn't forget?"

"Did I ever forget you? What do you think of this?" She placed a small woolly object in Chichi's outstretched hands.

"Look, Chichi, this is a little bear. What will you give me for the little bear?"

"I'll give you a bear hug," and Chichi, suiting the action to the words, gave her sister a big hug as Alouette knelt down to her level.

"For the rest of you," Alouette said, as the twins Jacques and Noel gathered around, "there are candy bears. Chichi rates something extra because she has a cold and has been such a good girl about taking her medicine."

Alouette produced a striped paper bag and presented each of the three-year-old twins with a chocolate bear.

"Now here is one for you, Chichi, and one for André and, yes, one for you, too," she laughed as Armand, the big farm dog, came over and sniffed at the bag.

"Poor Minou and her kittens. They don't like candy, do they?" Chichi asked, turning her eyes to the hearth in front of the big fireplace where the mother cat was busily engaged in giving her small kittens a bath.

"No, cats don't like candy," Alouette said, removing her cloak.

"Why don't cats . . ." Chichi started to say, then changed the subject as she peered down at the hearth. "Oh, Alouette, you dropped something out of your pocket." She stooped and was about to pick up the object, but Alouette was too quick for her. For on the hearth lay the mysterious cat's eye ring on its golden chain.

"What did you drop?" asked the curious Chichi.

"Nothing you would be interested in." Alouette hastily picked up the ring and replaced it in her pocket. She was thankful that Chichi and not André had seen the ring fall to the stone hearth.

But Chichi proved to have a larger bump of curiosity than Alouette realized.

"Let me see," Chichi demanded, stamping her foot.

"No. It is nothing you would be interested in," her sister said, trying to assume a casual air. "Let's talk about the little woolly bear, shall we? What will you name him?" she asked, to divert her sister.

"What color would you say he is?" Chichi asked.

"Well, I think he is brown, a sort of cinnamon color."

"Cinnamoo?"

"Cinnamon."

"Cinnamoo!" Chichi insisted.

"Well, then, have it your way. The bear's name is Cinnamoo," said Alouette laughing. "And now it's time to set the table."

"I'll help you," said Chichi. "I'll get the blue mugs for the milk."

"Of course," Alouette said in a matter-of-fact tone, and her sister's small hands moved about the table setting the mugs in their proper places.

"My goodness! Chichi, you are growing up,"

Alouette said, hugging her. "You can set the table as well as I can."

"I'm a big girl now," said the five-year-old proudly.

"A very big girl, almost a young lady," Alouette agreed, laughing.

There was heavy stamping of feet on the stoop outside the door now, and Grandpère came in. His bearded face was wreathed in smiles and he was rubbing his mittened hands together cheerfully as he brought a breath of the cold air into the room.

"I tell you the Christmas trees in the back lot are more beautiful than they have ever been," he said, beaming at his large family who, now that he had arrived, were taking their places around the long table with the red-and-white checkered cloth.

"To come from the cold, outside world into this warm, pleasant room, to know that we are all together, well and happy, makes one glad that the old customs never change on the Island of Orléans. Eh, Mother?" And Grandpère seated himself at the head of the long table while they all bowed their heads as he, in the custom of French Canadians, offered thanks for their blessings this winter evening. Only the baby, asleep in her cradle, was missing from the table.

When the prayer was over, Grandpère spoke to Papa. "I tell you, Noel, you have done us all proud. Six little ones in twelve years. A good record, even for French Canada, where the cradle is never empty."

"And who knows, there may be six more, eh?"

"Hush!" Grandmère said, looking at her husband over her spectacles, as Maman turned a rosy pink. "Hush! Let's be thankful for the six we have," the old lady said, ladling the fragrant, steaming soup into big, blue bowls.

"And what did you do today, Alouette?" Papa asked, to change the subject.

"The little hooked rug I took to Henri Tremblay's store is sold," Alouette said.

"But why didn't you tell us before?" her mother asked.

Why indeed? In the excitement of meeting the Northern Traveler and receiving the cat's eye ring, Alouette had quite forgotten about the little hooked rug.

"It was bought by a lady from the United States."

"Did she give a pretty penny for it?" The starched frill on Grandmère's cap seemed to bristle with interest. Grandmère knew for sure why her granddaughter worked so many hours after school to make the beautiful little rugs.

"Seven whole dollars," Alouette answered.

"What are you going to do with all that money?" André asked.

"Ask me no questions and I'll tell you no lies," she said laughing.

But she did not answer his question, for Alouette had a secret fund that none of the other children knew about. Alouette Robinette was saving her money to buy the small pony and little sleigh she wanted so very much, so she worked very hard making her little hooked rugs.

The rugs were pictures of the simple farm life of her native land. Alouette drew the designs herself, and under her grandmother's watchful eye, dyed the strips of cloth different colors, then wound each color into separate balls. After that the rugs were hooked on a wooden frame. They made excellent souvenirs for the many tourists who came from the United States, as they were true gifts from Canada.

But no one knew better than Alouette herself what a lot of hooked rugs she would have to make to reach her goal.

"Oh, my," she thought, "I'll be a hundred years

old before I get a pony and sleigh at the rate I am going now."

The chatter around the long table went on. When supper was over and the evening chores done, Alouette helped Maman put the little ones to bed.

She went to her own small room after this, and felt in the pocket of her red coat which hung in a wardrobe that had served her family ever since the first Robinettes had come from France to the New World.

She laid the ring on the washstand and prepared herself for bed.

And then at last she took the ring and chain over to the small glass lamp on the table beside her bed. The unwinking eye of the center stone glowed up at her.

"It is so beautiful, the cat's eye," she said, turning it this way and that. "Perhaps something inside the ring, something engraved there, will tell me who this stranger from Manitoba could be."

She examined the ring in the lamplight. "There is something engraved there . . . a name, I think . . . *M-i-z-p-a-h*," she spelled out. "My goodness, who would have a name like that? And why is all this such a secret?"

But the ring could give no clue. It only stared up at her with its unwinking eye as she tucked it into the lower drawer of the old wardrobe.

She blew out the light and peered through the small frosted panes of the dormer window. There was nothing out there in the long white road, nothing but snow that covered the north country with a soft white blanket.

Yet the whole world seemed filled with mystery to the young girl listening there. There was no sound, no sound at all save the snow tapping at her window pane, softly tapping out the strange word *"Mizpah, Mizpah, Mizpah,"* until at last she fell asleep.

CHAPTER 3

The White Sleigh

ALOUETTE's eleventh birthday came in white and sparkling.

She turned over sleepily in her warm bed. A terrific knocking and pounding were going on outside her door.

She sat up in bed. "What is it? It sounds as if General Wolfe's army is taking French Canada all over again!"

Much giggling came from the hallway.

"Well then!" She climbed from the warm bed and, walking gingerly on her heels to keep her feet off the cold floor as much as possible, flung open the door.

"Happy birthday!" chimed a chorus of merry voices.

"What . . . oh!"

"It's your *fête* day, Featherhead," André reminded her.

Alouette smiled and lifted Noel and Jacques, the three-year-old twins, to the bed. "Sit down then. I want a big hug from each of you. There is nothing so nice as having a lot of brothers and sisters, especially on your birthday."

"You want a hug from me?" André asked doubtfully.

"Why not? At least once a year." Alouette laughed as André gave her an awkward and hearty embrace.

"Now the twins . . . umm . . . ump! Those *were* big hugs. And Chichi . . . a big bear hug from you, a *real* bear hug, my little sister."

"I know a secret," Chichi said, after the birthday embraces were over.

"Well, it won't be a secret long, I bet, if you know it," Alouette said, tousling her little sister's hair.

"Maman and Grandmère have been baking something," Chichi said. "The candles are pink."

"You're not supposed to tell that," André said. "The cake with pink candles was to be a secret."

"Not if *that* one overhears it, André. There are

no secrets with our little Chichi around. Little pitchers have big ears!"

"Do I have big ears?" Chichi felt one small pink ear with interest.

"You are as big a featherhead as Alouette," said André. "You've got big ears and wheels in your head, and a big mouth."

"Oh no! Don't begin calling her Featherhead. There is no song that calls Chichi a featherhead, and she has *not* got a big mouth." But Alouette's defense was wasted on Chichi, who stood in front of the mirror over the washstand, stretching her mouth with her thumbs.

"I can make it bigger," she said proudly. "Look!"

But her dramatic gesture was interrupted. "Children! Breakfast! You'd better hurry." It was Maman, standing at the foot of the stairs. "There are sausages and omelet."

"There will be no birthday cake for anyone if you don't all clear out while I dress," Alouette said, breaking the ice in the pink pitcher and pouring the water into the bowl on the washstand.

The mere mention of no birthday cake cleared the small room instantly. Her brothers and sisters clattered down the stairs.

A few moments later, Alouette emerged, dressed in dark blue wool and a starched white pinafore. Her taffy-colored hair was neatly braided into bristling pigtails, and her round face was shining from having been scrubbed with Maman's good soap.

The birthday breakfast was one fit for any queen or, as Maman said, "Fit for a birthday child."

Homemade sausages, an omelet light as a feather, wild strawberry jam, and bread freshly baked that morning, with good sweet butter. And, as always, the blue mugs of milk.

After breakfast the presents were eagerly opened.

"Such a business," Alouette kept muttering. There were hair ribbons from the twins, a knitted hood and jacket and woolen stockings from Grandmère, a light blue woolen dress and new pinafore from Maman.

There was even a pincushion in the shape of a tomato from Chichi, who explained, "I made some of it myself, and then I forgot what a tomato looked like, so Grandmère helped."

"I'll just bet she helped," said Alouette laughing. "And do you know what? I have always wanted a pincushion shaped like a tomato." Then,

"Oh, Grandpère," she cried, opening an oblong box, "patent leather shoes with cloth tops! I've never had a pair of patent leather shoes, only shoes that laced like a boy's."

André stepped forward then, and when Alouette opened his package she found a pink brush and comb that matched her pink washbowl and pitcher. There were more hair ribbons from Baby, light blue ones to match her new dress.

"Alouette—" Papa laid his hand on top of her head—"I can only *say* happy birthday until the postman comes. I wasn't going to tell you, but I sent to Montreal for your gift. It should have been here yesterday but surely it will come today."

"Oh, Montreal!" Alouette said excitedly. "It must be grand, something coming from Montreal."

"It is something befitting the eldest daughter of the Robinette family. Now no more about it until the postman comes."

At the first sound of the postman's whistle, Alouette seized the red shawl that hung on the peg behind the door and ran down the lane. But the postman shook his head. There was no package for Mademoiselle Alouette Robinette.

She returned to the house, trying not to show

her disappointment. But her grandmother read it in her face and came to the rescue.

"It is getting on toward noon now, my little one. Let's cut the birthday cake."

"The cake, oh!" Alouette gasped as Maman set the big cake, ablaze with eleven pink candles, on the table before her.

"Everyone gather around and watch Alouette blow out the candles," Grandmère called, and Robinettes appeared from every direction.

"Grandpère, birthday cake!" André called out the kitchen door.

"Well, coming then," called Grandpère from the barn.

"Fetch Papa from the Christmas tree grove," Grandmère said, and André scurried up the lane and back of the barn where Papa was inspecting the beautiful evergreens to see which would be ready for the Christmas market in Quebec.

"Now then," said Maman, "now that we are all here, shall we have milk with the cake?"

Everyone nodded as the blue mugs were set on the table.

"Now blow and make a wish, and if you blow out all the candles your dearest wish will come true," Maman told the birthday girl.

Alouette closed her eyes, puffed out her cheeks and blew . . . "Whoosh!" Every candle on the beautiful cake went out.

"You mustn't tell your wish," André warned her.

"Who knows that better than I do," his sister said.

"I know what she's wishing." Chichi's eyes sparkled with mischief. "Alouette is wishing for a little——"

"Hush!" her sister cautioned her. "Don't tell."

"It's something stylish, with bells on, anyhow," Chichi said, looking pleased with herself.

The day passed pleasantly. A very happy birthday, indeed, except for one thing—the missing package from Montreal.

"Maybe it's at the post office," Alouette said as the afternoon began to wane. "Could I hitch Herbert and go to the village, Papa?"

"Why not?" her father answered. "I'll hitch Herbert myself while you get bundled up. It is very cold outside."

So once again Alouette went *bumpity-bump* down the long white road. And once again Madame Durand peered through her window.

"There she goes, that one, lickety-split. It's a

wonder that old sledge doesn't fly into a thousand pieces."

But Alouette reached the store without incident or accident. She covered Herbert carefully with his woolen blanket, and went to the back of the store, which was the village post office.

"Henri," she asked breathlessly, "have you got a package for me?"

"Could it be from Montreal, this package?"

"Yes," Alouette nodded as Henri removed a large box from the shelf.

"Oh, I can't . . . I just can't wait until I get home." She tore the wrappings from the box.

"See, these are my birthday presents from Papa, Henri. Look at this, a new red coat with a fur collar, and a little round hat to match, and kid mittens trimmed in fur! I've never had any mittens but wool ones that Grandmère made."

"You will be the belle of Ste. Famille," said Henri, leaning over the counter, his mustache bristling with interest. "But I have a suggestion to make."

"What then?" Alouette asked.

"I would suggest that you head for home. Night is falling and the snow is deepening."

"So it is!" Alouette gathered up her treasures

and put them into the box. "Good night, Henri," she called out. Soon she was driving dependable old Herbert out of the village and onto the country road.

Without warning, Herbert stopped.

"Is something coming?" Alouette peered through the snow. "It's another sleigh!" She drew Herbert to the roadside to make room for the oncoming vehicle. "And what a sleigh!" The eyes of the little girl grew round with wonder.

Approaching her was a white sleigh, drawn by the most beautiful white horse she had ever seen. And the sleigh had a golden swan with a gracefully curving neck on each side of the dashboard.

Alouette looked at the beautiful horse with an expert eye. "My, look at that horse," she said to the back of Herbert's drooping head. "Look how she carries her head and tail high and proud. A thoroughbred if I ever saw one."

And now the sleigh came into full view. The driver was a lady of great beauty, and although she was bundled in furs and wore a little fur hat, Alouette could see that her hair was snow white.

On the other end of the seat sat a dark figure muffled in a black coat and hood. Between them sat a little girl somewhat younger than Alouette.

Alouette remembered her manners and waved a mittened hand. "Good evening, my lady," she called, "and to you, Madame, and to the little girl also. Welcome to Ste. Famille. May your stay be a pleasant one."

Then she thought, "The white-haired lady is as beautiful as the Snow Queen. The little girl is pretty, too, and they both smiled and waved back. But the old one, she is sour-faced and has no manners. . . . Well, Herbert, I guess they don't know our neighborly way of stopping to pass the time of day, eh? The old one is giving herself airs. Three hundred years the Robinettes have been in this country, but not one of us gives himself such airs!"

Now, as she went bumping down the road, Alouette was thinking of her grandmother's words.

"The natives are a proud people, proud of their accomplishments, proud to own their own farmland. We have kept our faith," Grandmère said, "and we have kept our language. We have kept the cradles filled. And our men, when they stand back of our ox-drawn ploughs, are clothed in wool from our own sheep, spun and woven and fashioned by the women in the family. There is no better life in the world than living on your own

land, free of debt and enjoying good health. This, indeed, is the creed of French Canada."

Thinking about this, Alouette was suddenly shaken out of it by a strange occurrence.

"For goodness sakes! Herbert, turn around and follow that white sleigh. I can't believe my eyes, but I think it has turned in the gates of Lonesome Manor."

This was an amazing thing, for no one ever went near the Manor except the old man who came at intervals to cut back the overgrown shrubbery and vines. Alouette drove back a little way and saw that she had not been mistaken about where the sleigh had gone.

"But they went through the gates, just like that," and Alouette attempted to snap the fingers of her mittened hand. "This day's doings, Herbert," she said, "are something no one will believe. Let's go home now."

So, bouncing and bumping in the old sledge, Alouette set off down the road toward the Robinette farmhouse. As she approached the open door of the barn, André was waiting for her as usual.

"Is that you, Alouette? I didn't hear you whistling."

"Whistling! My gracious, who could whistle when she has seen what I saw."

Alouette was out of the sledge now, unhitching the patient Herbert. There was a flat clanking sound from the bell on the harness as she hung it on the wall.

"What do you mean, what you saw?"

André stepped closer, placing a pail of good sweet oats beneath Herbert's soft velvet nose.

"You won't believe this," Alouette said breathlessly.

"Probably not. You are a good storyteller. You can make anything sound exciting."

"No!" Alouette stamped her foot. "I always tell the truth."

"Er . . . you *do* put a little extra frosting on the cake when you tell a story though," her brother reminded her. He began to sing:

"Featherhead, featherhead
Alouette, Alouette, ah!"

"Pooh! Stop that, or I'll tell you nothing."

"Tell away. I have stopped."

Alouette drew closer to her brother. "There are three strangers in town."

"Well?"

"A lady with snow-white hair, a sour-faced old one all in black, and a little girl with golden hair."

"Oh, yes," André nodded, "the Snow Queen in a golden coach, the old witch, and the fairy princess. I read that all in a story one time."

"I cross my heart, this is not a story. It is the truth. I cross my heart." Alouette made a pious gesture. "André, on my honor, they were not riding in a golden coach, they were riding in a white sleigh with two golden swans and jingling sleigh bells. And do you know what? They drove straight through the gates of Lonesome Manor."

"How do you know? You were going in the opposite direction."

"I turned Herbert around and followed them."

"But they could hear Herbert's bell. Didn't they look around?"

"Only the sour-faced old one dressed in black. She looked back over her shoulder as they went through the gates."

"Then what happened?"

"The white sleigh stopped at the stone veranda and the old man came out of the shadows and took the horse and sleigh away. After a moment, the white-haired lady and the little girl waited on the steps while the sour-faced old one put a key in the door.

"The door stuck at first, and even way out in the road I could hear it creaking as she pushed it open. Then the three of them went in, and I waited until someone lit a candle."

"And the old man?"

"Well, it was the old caretaker, the one who never speaks. He took the beautiful white horse and sleigh around the house and disappeared in the shadow of the windowless tower."

"The secret tower," André said, shivering a little. "You know what? There is a freezing, cold wind blowing in from the river." And André looked down the road where the old Manor stood back of its avenue of tall, pointing trees, as if the cold wind were coming from there.

Alouette hurried along behind him as he led the way out of the shadowy barn. It was a comforting sight to see the lamplight reflected in orange-colored squares on the snow as the winter evening deepened and the wind blew the snow into the fence corners.

The cheerful lamplight seemed to dispel the oncoming night and shut out the rest of the world. Even gloomy old Lonesome Manor down the road disappeared behind a veil of silently falling snow.

CHAPTER 4

The Snow Man

IN THE kitchen-parlor Maman was bending over the stove, lifting something from a big brass kettle.

"Does my nose deceive me, or are we really having partridge stewed with onions for my birthday dinner?" Alouette wrinkled her nose and sniffed the delicious cooking smells.

"It *is* partridge stewed with onions, the best Canada can provide," said Papa, after she had shown the presents from Montreal and they were all around the big table.

"And I hope my birthday child has found a good appetite out there in the snowy road," Maman declared, handing Alouette a heaping plate.

"You have never had to worry about my appetite," Alouette reminded her.

"Or any of the little Robinettes," Grandpère said, laughing. "Now the next *fête* day will be Christmas, the *fête* of the little Jesus, and that reminds me of work tomorrow after school for André . . . Christmas trees."

"Oh, is it time to pick out the trees for the Christmas market?" André always delighted in this task.

"The time has come. Tomorrow you and I will put a small notch in each tree that is to be cut for the market."

There was much talk about the Christmas market until supper was over. Then when the chores were done and the little ones put to bed, Maman and Papa went to visit some friends in the village.

André went to his room to work on the bright fishing tackle he was making, and Alouette sat down on a little stool on the hearth.

There was no one in the room but Grandmère and Grandpère, the big farm dog and the cat and her lively kittens.

Grandmère's knitting needles clicked busily while Grandpère read a seed catalogue from Quebec.

Alouette watched Grandmère's fingers flying over her work. "How many woolen socks has Grandmère made in her life, I wonder," she thought. "She has kept us all supplied all our lives."

It was very quiet in the comfortable old room. The snow-banked windowpanes made the scene look like a picture on a Christmas card. Everything seemed now to point to the *fête* of the little Jesus. But for the moment Alouette's thoughts were elsewhere.

"Grandmère?" Alouette broke the silence now.

"Yes dear."

"I saw something this afternoon as Herbert and I were coming from the post office. Something I have never before seen in Ste. Famille. I had a real adventure, Grandmère."

"Pooh! How could anyone have an adventure between this farmhouse and the village?"

"It was just at dusk," Alouette continued. "I met a white sleigh on the road."

Grandmère nodded, and did not look up from her knitting. "Many tourists take the trip around the Island. They rent sleighs in Quebec." Grandmère smiled. "They think the natives are quaint."

"No, this was not a tourist sleigh. It was

trimmed with golden swans and was drawn by a beautiful snow-white horse. It was a very stylish sleigh, and it jingled with bells. There was a lady in furs driving, and with her was a sour-faced old one, and a little girl not quite my age. Grandmère, this lady was different from anyone I have ever seen. She looked young, but still she had snow-white hair. And do you know what? The lady drove the white horse and sleigh through the gates of Lonesome Manor. They got out, and the old one opened the door. Then they all went in and someone lighted a lamp or a candle, and that is the last I saw of them."

Alouette looked up now. Her grandmother was staring at her. "Are you sure, Alouette? This is not a fairy tale you are making up to entertain me?"

"Cross my heart, every word is true."

Grandmère was staring at her husband now, and he had let the seed catalogue slide to the floor.

"Could . . . could it possibly be the white-haired Mamselle?" Grandmère said, almost in a whisper.

"Not unless you believe in ghosts," Grandpère said.

"Shh! Don't even mention such a thing as ghosts." Grandmère put a warning finger to her lips. "Little pitchers . . ."

54

"Yes, I know."

Alouette glanced from one face to the other, but no one explained what he was talking about.

Finally, after a long silence, Grandpère said in his hearty way, "Well, then, my little one, off to bed with you. Get your nightcap on."

And that was where the matter seemed to end.

But long after Maman and Papa came home, Alouette heard the four grownups talking. The murmur of their voices came up the stairway and into her small room, but she could not understand what the conversation was about.

Finally she heard Papa winding the clock and, later, banking the fire for the night. Then all was quiet. Alouette lay enveloped in silence, but she could not sleep.

Suddenly, the silence was broken by a muffled sound coming from the road. She rose and looked out into the moonlit white world. Through the frosted pane she saw a sledge passing. The sound she had heard was the thud of the horses' hoofs in the snow.

The sledge was piled high with something hidden beneath a bearskin robe. It seemed to be just an ordinary sledge, but it made not a sound save the dull *clop clop* of the horses' hoofs and the ghostly whoosh of the runners. There was not one tiny, tinkling bell. Alouette watched until its outline was lost in the thickly swirling snow.

Again the silence was broken suddenly, by a thundering clang.

"It's . . . someone using the iron knocker on the door of Lonesome Manor," she whispered to herself.

After this all was quiet, until once again she heard the soft thud of horses' hoofs in the snow. The sledge was returning, empty now. It was on its way back to Quebec.

There was *nothing* in it now. Nothing but the driver, making his way home over the lonely, snow-covered road. Alouette put her head down again, her mind dark and fuzzy with thoughts of Lonesome Manor and the eerie, silent sledge.

In the morning, she realized that what she had seen was probably the sledge carrying all the possessions of the new occupants of Lonesome Manor. But it certainly was a strange time to be making a delivery.

Now it was morning and Alouette stood waiting at the gate, listening for the friendly *scrape, scrape* of the Snow Man's shovel. The Snow Man, as everyone on the Island of Orléans knows, is a very important person. It is he who keeps the roads cleared all through the long, cold Northern winter, going through each of the villages that wreath the Island like a string of bright beads.

But even more important to the snowbound farm people of the Island, it is the Snow Man who brings news and carries it away with him.

Alouette held the red shawl tightly beneath her chin and tried to look through the snow. At last the familiar scraping sound she had been listening for came to her ears, and then the genial Snow Man, his horse, and his big blue sledge appeared.

Now he was driving his big blue sledge piled high with snow toward Alouette's gate.

" 'Allo, 'allo, 'allo," the Snow Man called cheerfully, waving a mittened hand. "Do you know what day this is, my little one?"

"Yes, of course. It is St. Catherine's Day, Edmond. Everyone knows that. It is good luck to be the first to see the Snow Man on this day.

"What's the news, Edmond?" Alouette asked this politely, although she herself was bursting with news and questions about the mysterious things going on.

"Let me see now." The Snow Man laid a mittened finger beside his nose, and appeared to be lost in deep thought . . . "Well, there are a number of new babies on the Island."

"Yes, there are always new babies. In French Canada the cradle is never empty. I wouldn't call that news."

"Look here!" For once, the Snow Man appeared to be serious. "Look here, Alouette Robinette. New babies are important." He spread his arms wide, as if the new babies encompassed the world. "It is the duty of every French Canadian girl to help her parents in the first place, then in good time to get married and bring up a family of her own.

"You, yourself, will be taking great pride in the fact that you are bringing up a good Christian family. All in good time, that is," he said as an afterthought, remembering that Alouette had just turned eleven.

"All in good time, Edmond," Alouette said laughing. "A girl must first find herself a husband."

"You will find a good man," said the Snow Man, wagging his head. "Your Grandmère found one, and your Maman found one also. One of the best in the Island. The Robinettes are all good men. They have been so for generations. It is a great

pity your cousin Jacques went away. He was as
fine a man as ever was born here, an honest man,
dependable and a hard worker. Always happy and
whistling."

Alouette nodded. "And very handsome. I want
to ask you something, though."

"Ask away then, but make it brief. I am a government official. I must keep the King's Highway
cleared."

"Who knows that better than I do? We couldn't
get along without you," Alouette said.

"What was it you wanted to ask me then?"

"I wanted to ask you if you knew someone was living at Lonesome Manor."

"No!" The Snow Man shook his head. "That is not possible."

"It is possible," Alouette insisted. "A beautiful lady with snow-white hair, a sour-faced old lady, and a little girl drove into the gates at dusk yesterday. I saw them. They were in a white sleigh trimmed with golden swans, and the horse was white, too."

"Even more impossible," declared the Snow Man, crossing himself.

He stepped close to Alouette. "Listen, my little one. It is sinful to believe in ghosts."

"Pooh! Who believes in them?"

"Well, then, see that you do not speak of them," said the Snow Man, eying her sharply.

"Why . . . Edmond? Why should you say a thing like that to me?" Alouette asked.

"Because you are telling me you have seen a ghost right here on this very road, between your father's farm and Lonesome Manor."

"No, no, not a ghost, a real lady."

"Listen, then, what you say you saw was a beautiful white-haired lady, driving a white sleigh decorated with golden swans? And the gold and white sleigh was drawn by a fine, high-stepping white horse? Is that what you are telling me?"

"Yes. And there was a sour-faced old one dressed in black, and a little girl in the sleigh with the lady."

The Snow Man removed his woolen cap and scratched his head. "Little girl, eh? That is odd."

"What is odd about it?"

"Well . . . the . . . little girl . . . no one ever spoke of her."

"Why should they?"

"Who knows?" Edmond replaced his cap. "I will tell you this, though. It is impossible for you to have seen that sleigh driven by a white-haired lady go through the gates of Lonesome Manor."

"But I did."

"Listen carefully then, and I will tell you something."

The Snow Man leaned closer. "There was a time when the white-haired lady lived at the old manor house. It was not called Lonesome Manor then. The white-haired lady was brought there by her father, a widower from Scotland. She lived there with him and her old Scottish nurse."

"Yes." Alouette nodded.

"The lady was beautiful, with long blonde hair,

so blonde that she was called the white-haired Mamselle, even when she first came here as a young girl."

"The very one I saw, Edmond."

"No, listen to me. You could not have seen the white-haired Mamselle driving the white sleigh and white horse through the Manor gates."

"How can you be so sure?"

"Because," and Edmond took out his handkerchief and blew his nose violently, "because, my little one, the old Scottish nurse and the white-haired Mamselle are both dead."

"The white-haired Mamselle? She is dead?"

"Dead."

And the Snow Man turned and made his way down the road toward Lonesome Manor.

CHAPTER 5

A New Friend

ALOUETTE DECIDED there was no use asking Grandmère any questions about the white-haired Mamselle, and certainly no use in telling her that the Snow Man had tried to convince her she had seen a ghost.

But Grandpère had mentioned ghosts too, when Grandmère had spoken of the white-haired Mamselle. But of course Grandpère had only said: " . . . unless you believe in ghosts," and then Grandmère had shushed him and put her finger to her lips.

"Well then," Alouette decided, "I couldn't talk to anyone in the family today about anything."

As Alouette reached the foot of the stairs the next morning the kitchen-parlor was in a hubbub. "My goodness, what is going on down here? Everyone is talking at once," she said as she sat down at the breakfast table.

"We are all going to Quebec, all except you," Chichi informed her excitedly. Maman and Grandmère were going to shop, Papa and Grandpère to select their spot in the Christmas market to display their trees.

"What's wrong with me? Don't I belong in the family any more? There's no school today." Alouette looked at her mother curiously.

"That's just it, dear, there's no school today. I thought if you wouldn't mind staying home with the baby, Grandmère and I could get so much more Christmas shopping done."

"Of course I don't mind, Maman."

"Well, the bread is in the outside oven. Take it out in an hour. Give Baby her lunch and . . ."

"Oh, Maman! I know how to do all those things. Go on to Quebec, all of you, and have a good time."

Soon they were on their way, bundled to their noses under the bearskin robe.

When Herbert and the big sledge disappeared from view, Alouette left the window where she had waved them away and went into Maman's room. Baby was fast asleep in her wooden cradle. Alouette went up to her room to look again at the cat's eye ring given her by the Northern Traveler, a ring she could not even show to her own family. "What good does that do me, and who is this mysterious person in faraway Manitoba?"

Downstairs Armand began to bark.

"What's wrong?" Alouette called out, but the big dog continued to bark and mutter.

"You'll wake the baby up, Armand. Quiet!" she called from the head of the stairs. She went back into the room and put the ring away in the drawer of the wardrobe.

This time Armand was quiet, but she heard another sound in the lane by the barn. It was the soft whinny of a horse.

"Somebody has left his barn door open," Alouette thought, as she hurried down the stairs.

"My goodness, it's the white horse from Lonesome Manor! What will I do?" Alouette spoke aloud to herself. "Well, there is only one thing to do, take the horse back where she came from. This horse is not a ghost. She is real."

"Whoa!" she called out from the doorway, and the horse stood still.

Alouette went to a basket in the pantry and got a big red apple. Then she went out to the lane, putting on her red coat and hood as she approached the horse.

"You are the most beautiful horse in the world," she said, offering the apple on the palm of her hand. "And you are real and as for all this silly talk about ghosts down there . . . pooh! Who's afraid?"

Thoughts were buzzing around in Alouette's head like bees.

"I wonder how she got out of the stable, and through those heavy iron gates? They must be leaving the gates open now," she thought.

Alouette took a long, deep breath. "Well, come into the barn," she said softly, and opened the sliding doors of the big comfortable barn. The white horse followed her through the door, still munching the apple. "Now I'll get a halter on you and take you home, eh?"

Alouette looked down the lane. "But the Snow Man has not cleared the road."

The horse stopped dutifully while Alouette buckled on her snowshoes, which had been thrust into a snowdrift and were standing upright beside the door.

Soon the small figure in the red coat, plodding along on snowshoes, led the beautiful horse down the white road.

"I never thought I'd be going in here," Alouette thought, as she led the horse through the open iron gates. She removed her snowshoes and stood them in the snow, then mounted the steps and lifted the heavy iron knocker. It fell with the same thundering clang she had heard in the night when the sleigh from Quebec had stopped at the old house.

"What's wanted? Who's there?" called a crotchety voice.

"It's me, Alouette Robinette, and I don't want anything."

"Go away then, and stop wasting my time."

"I can't go away."

"Why not?"

"I . . . I . . . can't go away because I have the white horse."

"What? What did you say?" There was the sound of a heavy footfall in the hall. The door swung open on its creaking hinges.

"The white horse, Colette? Why did you take her? Where did you get her?" The speaker was the sour-faced one, and it was evident that she regarded Alouette Robinette with deep suspicion.

"Oh, no, Madame. I did not take the horse away. She came to my house. Right up the lane she came, without even a halter on."

"Humph!" said the woman eying her suspiciously. "She seems to have a halter on now. I'll give that old caretaker a piece of my mind. I will indeed!"

"Well, *I* put it on her," Alouette explained. "The halter belongs to Herbert."

"Who is Herbert? And what do you mean, *you* put it on her? Do you know that Colette is a high-spirited Arabian horse? She will hardly stand for anyone touching her except her mistress, who loves and understands horses very well. *You* put the halter on Colette? A likely story indeed!"

"Well, I love and understand horses too," Alouette said. "It is well known on the Island that I understand and love horses, and know how to handle them. And you, Madame, can take or leave it." She added as an afterthought, "I did not have to return the horse. I could have just let her wander away. If you will call her mistress I would be pleased to have her lead her to the coachhouse, and then give me back Herbert's halter, and let me go home."

"And where might home be, and who, I ask again, is Herbert? You seem to have spirit," said the old one.

Alouette pointed toward the farmhouse. "The second house down there, Madame. And Herbert is my father's big brown farm horse. One of the best on the Island."

"So *you* are a Robinette," the old woman muttered. "And you are the one we met on the road the night we came home."

"Home?" Alouette said with surprise.

But before Alouette could recover from her surprise, a voice called from the inside of the house. "Who is it, Nana?"

It was then that the lady came through the open front door of Lonesome Manor. Alouette gasped. She was the most beautiful lady she had ever seen. Her face was pink and white and smooth, unlike the suntanned skin of the farm women. And over her snow-white hair the lady wore a black lace scarf. Her eyes were blue, but there was a strangeness about them that held Alouette's attention. They seemed to be looking at something far away, as if she were lost in a dream.

"This child," said the sour-faced one, "says she found Colette wandering in the farm lane."

69

"Oh Colette, how did you get out?" The lady with the white hair laid her cheek against the horse's velvet nose. Then she turned to Alouette. "How can I ever thank you, my dear? Colette is very dear to me."

"You don't have to thank me," Alouette said. "I love horses too. I drive my father's farm horse, Herbert, all the time. Herbert is not stylish like Colette, but he is gentle and you can trust him. Herbert never runs away," she said pointedly, and the lady laughed aloud.

"You know," she said earnestly, looking at Alouette, "I don't believe I have ever been as happy to see anyone as I am to see you."

"Me?" Alouette said. "How can that be?"

"Well, you see, I have a little girl too, and I have been afraid she was going to be very lonely in this old house with just Nana and me. I wonder if you could come here and play with her sometimes?"

"I'd like to have a new friend."

"Well then, I'll call her. Maria?"

"Yes, Mamselle," a voice answered from inside the house. Then the little fair-haired girl appeared in the doorway.

"Mamselle!" Alouette's heart thumped against

70

her ribs. The little girl had called the white-haired lady Mamselle. Could this possibly be the white-haired Mamselle after all?

But the lady was speaking again. "Maria, this is the little girl we met the other evening driving the sledge. She brought Colette home. Colette got out of the stable. I guess she was lonely too."

"Will you come in and play with me?" Maria asked eagerly.

"Come in? Oh, but I can't! I left the baby at home alone. I forgot about her for a little bit, but I must go. She might wake up and be frightened." Alouette hastily buckled on her snowshoes.

"Well, thank you again, my dear. But you haven't told me your name," the white-haired lady said.

"My name is Alouette Robinette."

As she told her name, the sour-faced old one looked at the white-haired lady sharply, but if the name meant anything at all to her, Mamselle did not show it.

"I don't know what I would do without Colette," said the lady. "Wait, I'll give you back your halter. Colette will follow me anywhere."

She was holding the halter out to Alouette, but for a moment Alouette was too dumbfounded to take it. She was staring at the white-haired lady's hands, for on the third finger of the left hand was a gold ring with flashing green stones and an unblinking cat's eye in the center.

The ring was an exact match for the one the Northern Traveler had given to Alouette the evening he stopped her at her father's gate. What was it he had said then? "There is but one other . . ."

Like someone in a trance, Alouette took the halter from the lady's outstretched hand. "I must go. Baby might be awake," she stammered at last.

"Goodby, and remember your promise to come back and play with me soon," Maria reminded her. "And maybe I could get some snowshoes too."

"Yes, of course I'll come." But Alouette was so puzzled over the mystery of the two rings she scarcely knew what she was saying.

"It couldn't possibly be my ring," she thought, as she went into the farmhouse where the baby was still asleep. But to make sure Alouette went upstairs and opened the wardrobe drawer.

"Well, there it is."

And sure enough, her own ring lay in the drawer just as she had left it. Then there *was* another one like it, just as the Northern Traveler had told her.

CHAPTER 6

Grandmère's Story

IT WAS beginning to snow harder as Alouette stood, nose pressed to the windowpane, waiting for the sound of the brass harness bell that
would tell her that Herbert was bringing the
Robinette family home from Quebec in the big
sledge. She had the soup kettle steaming on the
big stove, and the table set for supper. Now there
was nothing to do but wait and wait until she could
tell them about the white horse and her visit to
Lonesome Manor.

At last the sound she had been waiting for
came . . . *ting-a-ling-a-ling* . . . and Herbert and
the big wooden sledge turned into the lane.

There was a chorus of voices on the stoop outside as Alouette opened the door and spoke to the children who had run ahead of their elders.

"Sweep the snow off your boots, every one of you," she admonished. "Only the twins, I'll sweep yours first. And now we'll go into the house and have a nice, hot meal, eh?"

She led them all into the brightly lighted, warm kitchen-parlor.

Chichi crinkled her small button nose with pleasure. "Umm . . . it smells nice in here."

"It is nice," Alouette agreed. "We will have a good warm supper, eh?"

Then she stopped talking for a moment, remembering the stranger on snowshoes she had met in the dusk only a few evenings ago. He had used those very same words: "A good warm supper, eh?"

But her thoughts were interrupted by the arrival of the other members of the family.

"You all look like bundled up Eskimos," Alouette said laughing, as they began taking off woolen jackets and hoods, knitted woolen scarfs and mittens. A breath of the cold winter evening still lingered around them.

"And just as hungry as bears. And I'll bet Alouette Robinette, that eleven-year-old young lady of the family, has something good to eat for us, something fit for a king, eh?" And Grandpère came over and pinched her cheek.

"Yes, a stew with meat and vegetables, and I took the bread out of the outside oven as Maman told me and it is still warm, and the baby is fine."

But although she was bursting with news, it was not until they were all seated around the table that Alouette had a chance to tell it.

"And what did you do with yourself besides tending the oven and the baby, and getting supper?" André asked. "Was it a long, lonesome day?"

Alouette drew a deep breath and, looking straight at André, spoke in an offhand manner. "Oh, no, it was not lonesome at all. I went visiting."

"Visiting without a horse and sleigh?" André looked at his sister with unbelieving eyes. "Surely you didn't go to see that nosy Madame Durand. She is our nearest neighbor, but not our dearest neighbor."

"Oh no, not Madame Durand." Alouette buttered a slice of the warm dark bread with an elaborately casual air. "And I went on snowshoes."

"Where then?" André asked.

Alouette laid the slice of bread on her plate. "Oh, just down to Lonesome Manor."

"Featherhead, you are making that up!" her brother said accusingly.

"Pooh!" said his sister, tossing her head.

"Stop, André! Let Alouette tell us," her father said sternly.

"Well—" Alouette rolled her eyes and took a second deep breath. This was the moment she had been waiting for. "Well, the white horse I told you about the other evening got out of the stable down there and came up our lane."

Everyone was silent now.

"And I just put on my coat and hood and snowshoes and put a halter on her and led her back to Lonesome Manor. The old one with the sour face came to the door. She was very cross at first. She would not believe the horse had run away. But the white-haired lady came to the door and thanked me for returning Colette . . . that is the white horse's name. And the little girl came out and said she would like to have me for a friend. The white-haired lady said I would hear from her again, and then I came home and the baby was still asleep, and . . . and that is all."

But apparently that was not all, for when she looked at them Grandpère, Grandmère, Maman and Papa were all staring at each other as though

78

a ghost had just walked into the room. You could have heard a pin drop.

Finally Maman broke the silence. "Do you think it could possibly be . . . ?"

Grandmère nodded. "It sounds very much like it, but I don't see how such a thing is possible." She turned to her granddaughter. "Was the white-haired lady very beautiful?"

"Oh, yes, beautiful and small, with a pink and white skin and blue eyes. She had a black lace scarf over her head."

"The white-haired Mamselle," Maman answered. "She always wore a black lace scarf. That is called a *mantilla*, Alouette. They are worn by the ladies of Spain, and many French ladies wear them to church."

But this seemed to be the end of the matter, at least for the moment. After the younger children had said their prayers and were safely tucked in bed, Maman spoke to Alouette, who was working away at her small hooked rug.

"Put away your work, Alouette. Grandmère has something to tell you."

"Is it something about Lonesome Manor?"

Maman nodded. "Yes, it is a long story."

"Well, to begin at the very beginning," Grandmère said, "the old Manor house was built by a Scottish officer by the name of McPherson, who had been given a title and land grant by General Wolfe. A number of the Highlanders were so honored for their bravery in helping capture Quebec many years ago.

"French Canada was a new world then and Indians roamed about. Not friendly ones, as are the Hurons in Lorette, but savage Indians who would stop at nothing.

"Well then, this McPherson, or the Laird, as he was called, built the Manor house down the road. He built it to look as much like the old castles that stand on the lonely moors of Scotland as was possible. They say it was beautiful then, standing in the midst of the wilderness.

"Then the Laird of the Manor went back to Scotland for a visit and returned with a young wife to live in the great house.

"As time went on, the roving bands of Indians became more savage. So savage that they would even steal the children of the white settlers, sometimes holding them for ransom, sometimes raising them as members of their own tribe.

"One of the Laird's children barely missed this dreadful fate, and in saving the little girl the Laird lost his own life. He fell into the hands of the Indians and nothing was ever heard of him again."

"And the white-haired Mamselle, what of her?" Alouette interrupted.

"That part of the story will come all in good time," Grandmère replied.

"Time passed, two years in fact, and the Laird's wife waited, hoping and praying for his return. Then the Indian attacks grew more frequent. The lady of the Manor had no choice but to take her children out of the New World. They returned to Scotland. It had been rumored that the first Laird kept a treasure hidden in the Manor but if so, no one ever found it.

"It seems that at this time in Scotland the estate of the elder brother was inherited by the brother next in line. So some time later, another young Laird came from Scotland. He married a French-Canadian girl from Quebec. It is amazing how many Scottish and French-Canadian families are related," Grandmère added, smiling.

"Yes, I know that," Alouette said. "There is a girl at school whose name is Annette McDonald, and she speaks nothing but French."

"Well, then," Grandmère continued, "the Manor house was open again. Great parties were held there. For several generations it was occupied by heirs of the McPherson families.

"It was the custom every year to entertain the native gentry with a great Christmas party. Hundreds of candles and wreaths of holly decked the halls. Venison and partridge . . . everything the heart could wish . . . were served while the Yule log burned in the fireplace of the great hall. And then, as sometimes happens to families, the last heir to the Manor who was Canadian-born, died. And once again the Manor house stood vacant."

"But the last Laird, Grandmère? How did he come by Lonesome Manor?"

Grandmère paused for a moment. "That is a sad story but one which I think should be told to you.

"The last Laird, the very last of the line, came across from Scotland. He was a widower, and he brought with him his small fair-haired daughter, and her Scottish nurse."

Alouette gasped. She felt as though she were gradually fitting the pieces of a puzzle together.

"Once again," Grandmère continued, "the old Manor house came to life. At this time it was the liveliest place on the Island. The lovely blonde daughter was growing up. Her hair was so fair that no one called her by her real name. She was known far and wide as the white-haired Mamselle.

"Such a one, of course, had many suitors," Grandmère went on, "but she had eyes for only one. And so they became betrothed. Three times the banns were published, as is the custom, and the betrothal announced to all the townspeople by the town crier.

"Everyone was looking forward to the wedding party that was to be held at the Manor house, after the good priest had read the marriage ceremony at the church."

"And then?"

"Well, as suddenly as that, the Laird sickened and died, just before the wedding."

"How terrible!" Alouette covered her face with her hands.

"But even worse," Grandmère continued, "were the things that happened later. The Laird had requested that he be laid to rest beside his wife in Scotland. So the white-haired Mamselle and her Scottish nurse set out on their sad journey. But they never reached Scotland. There was a terrific storm at sea and all aboard the ship were lost. It was reported that not a soul survived."

"Part of this the Snow Man told me, Grandmère. He said the white-haired Mamselle and her nurse were dead."

"Yes, that is the message that came back to us, but now I wonder . . ."

"But then, the young man she was to marry, what became of him?"

Grandmère removed her spectacles and brushed her handkerchief across her eyes. "This is the most difficult part of all to tell, Alouette. The young man, beside himself with grief, set out for a lumber camp in the far north woods. Perhaps this was a foolish thing to do. One cannot run away from sorrow. But the young man set out on this dangerous journey alone, and on snowshoes, in the dead of winter."

"And then?"

"Well, he went . . . astray." The dread word was almost whispered.

"Oh, no, not astray!" Alouette exclaimed, for in the north woods the word "astray" means lost in the deadly winter forest.

"Yes, somehow he must have taken a wrong turn, and to this day no one has ever known what happened to him."

"And who . . . who was this young man?" Alouette asked, breaking the silence.

"His name . . . his name . . . was Jacques Robinette."

"My own *cousin,* Jacques Robinette?"

Grandmère nodded. "Do you remember him? He was an orphan. He lived in this house."

"Yes, of course I remember him. I knew he went on a journey, but no one ever told me where or why."

"Well, you were such a little girl, as small as Chichi. It is not a happy story. But," Grandmère continued, "make no mistake, Jacques Robinette was a happy young man. He was always laughing and whistling . . . whistling so his sweetheart, Alouette, would know he was on the way to the Manor house."

"Alouette? The white-haired Mamselle's name was Alouette?"

"Yes, you are her namesake. You were named after the beautiful white-haired Mamselle, the last heir to the Manor.

"So that is the story of Lonesome Manor," Grandmère said, rising.

"No, not quite." Alouette tugged at her sleeve. "What was the tune he used to whistle, Cousin Jacques, when he went down the road to see his sweetheart?"

"Featherhead, Featherhead, Alouette, what else?"

"He called *her* Featherhead?" Alouette asked in amazement.

"Yes, for two reasons. Because she had been named Alouette after one of her French relatives, and because her lovely hair was so very light, light as a feather, Jacques used to say."

For the first time during the story, Grandmère smiled. "And when the white-haired Mamselle heard him coming, she would run down the path to the iron gate whistling 'Frère Jacques.' Alouette and Jacques, you see, belong together."

Alouette remembered something now. The Northern Traveler had said almost these same words. "Alouette and Jacques belong together."

"Grandmère, do you believe the lady down at the Manor is the white-haired Mamselle?"

But before Grandmère could answer, there was a knock on the door.

Alouette opened the door. The old man who took care of Lonesome Manor handed her a note. He did not speak, but simply stood there and waited.

The note bore her name, *Mademoiselle Alouette Robinette*. Alouette opened the envelope and read aloud: "You are invited to take tea at the Manor house Thursday afternoon at four." The note was unsigned.

"Thursday! Why that is tomorrow . . . oh . . . what shall I do? Maman, Grandmère, take tea at the Manor house tomorrow! Oh, what a day!"

Maman went to the door and spoke to the silent man on the doorstep. "Mademoiselle Alouette will be delighted to take tea at the Manor house tomorrow at four," she said.

The man nodded and set off down the lane.

"I can't believe it yet," Alouette said excitedly. "Tea at the Manor house. I am invited to take tea at Lonesome Manor! Grandmère," she said, "do you believe that there is a mystery about the windowless tower?"

"The Laird's Treasure, as it is called?" Grandmère said, softly.

"Yes, do you believe these things may be true after all?"

Her grandmother looked at her over her spectacles. Always before she had said these stories were old wives' tales. Now she picked up her knitting and sat down by the fire. But then she let the knitting fall into her lap and shook her head. "Who knows, my little one, who knows?" she said.

CHAPTER 7

Afternoon Tea

AT EXACTLY twenty-five minutes to four on Thursday afternoon Alouette was ready to start out for Lonesome Manor to take tea. But with whom? There had been no name signed to the invitation, although it had been written on heavy cream-colored paper in a fine, delicate hand, in lavender ink.

Alouette sat stiffly on a big chair in the kitchen-parlor, gazing through the frosted window at the white world beyond. She was dressed in her Sunday best, starched white pinafore over her bright blue wool dress. Her taffy-colored pigtails were braided so tightly they seemed to pull her eyebrows upward.

She wore her new red birthday coat, kid mittens and the patent leather shoes with cloth tops, but the crowning glory was the small round hat of red felt. It was the first hat Alouette had ever owned. In the farm country a young girl wears a woolen hood in winter, and in summer a scarf serves as a head covering when she goes to church.

"Don't forget, dear. Mind your manners. Leave your boots on the veranda. Take off your coat and mittens in the house."

"And the hat, Maman?"

"Oh, surely! By all means leave the hat on. It is stylish to wear a hat to tea."

This was good news to Alouette, for to her the little red hat represented the fashionable world of Montreal.

"Are you sure, Papa?" she asked for the fifth time. "Are you sure Herbert is curried and brushed enough? I love Herbert, but his coat gets shaggy in winter, and he doesn't look very stylish."

"Herbert not stylish? What a thought," Papa exclaimed. "Herbert is groomed, my lady, to the Queen's taste, and his best red blanket is folded and in the sleigh, ready to put over him while your ladyship is in the Manor house taking tea."

Alouette knew her father was teasing her, but

she was very serious about the afternoon's doings.

It had been decided, after much family consultation, that it would be proper for Alouette to drive alone to the Manor, for there was nothing in the invitation to indicate what time the tea would be over.

Now at last, as Alouette sat stiffly watching the clock, the hands moved to ten minutes to four. This was the exact time that she had decided upon to start. It took seven minutes to drive down the road to Lonesome Manor. She had timed it to the exact minute. And at this very moment, Herbert's bell jingled in the lane as André brought him to the stoop.

"Cinderella, your coach awaits," André announced as he came clumping into the room.

"Oh, thank you." And in less time than it takes to tell, the entire Robinette family was assembled at the stoop, waving her on her way as the old sledge went bumping and thumping down the long white road.

At three minutes to four, the sledge swept through the big iron gates and stopped at the stone steps that led to the front door of Lonesome Manor.

Alouette turned to the silent caretaker who was

waiting to conduct Herbert and the sledge to the stable. "Please be sure to put his blanket on," she cautioned him. "Herbert is very particular."

The caretaker cocked an eyebrow at the big black farm horse and nodded.

Alouette slipped her boots off and set them neatly beside the door. The time had come at last to lift the heavy knocker. Her heart was beating wildly as the knocker clanged. What would she find in there, she wondered. She, Alouette, in her very best dress and in her red coat and small red hat, was about to enter Lonesome Manor!

There was a patter of footsteps inside, and the door opened. Maria smiled a welcome. "Come in. I've been waiting for you." She held the heavily carved door open, and Alouette stepped into what seemed to her like an enchanted castle.

"Oh! I never dreamed the old Manor was so beautiful inside."

She let Maria take her red coat and fur mittens like one in a trance.

"We love it here," Maria said. "Mamselle has been happier here than any place we have ever lived. She says it really does seem like home."

"It seems like a fairy castle to me," Alouette said, as she looked around the big hall.

A fire was burning in the big stone fireplace, making the great room cheery, but Alouette was used to snapping wood fires. What attracted her eye most were the unusual stairways. Two sets of marble steps carpeted in red curved upward to a wide landing. And at the back of this landing, standing against a carved Gothic panel that came to a point at the top, stood a huge grandfather clock.

"I never saw two stairways leading to one place," Alouette said. "And the clock against the panel . . . is it very old?"

But before Maria could answer her question, the old clock cleared its throat and boomed out four o'clock. Alouette looked at its pointing hands and smiled with appreciation. She was exactly on time, and it seemed to her that the friendly old clock had gone out of its way to tell her so, and to say "Welcome, Alouette, welcome to Lonesome Manor."

"We are having tea in here." Maria led the way to a pleasant room at the side of the great hall, where a small marble fireplace threw out a cozy and welcoming cheer.

"Could I take your hat?" Maria asked politely.

"Oh no, no, Maman said . . ." then Alouette

stopped. Who was she, a farm girl, to tell Maria what was fashionable.

"I like the hat," Maria said. "Would you let me try it on?"

"Of course."

Maria tried on the little round hat and looked in the mirror over the mantel.

"It is becoming," Alouette said, and Maria nodded and handed it back to her.

"Yes, but it is more becoming to you."

"I'll tell you a secret," Alouette said, putting the hat back on. "This is the first hat I ever had. Papa got it in Montreal."

"Your father has good taste," Maria said admiringly.

"Yes, but he didn't go to Montreal after it. You see, he picked it out of the catalogue," Alouette said truthfully.

"Mamselle lets me go with her when she buys things. Would you like to go shopping with us sometime?" Maria suggested.

"Would I!" Alouette's eyes were sparkling with anticipation. "But—" she leaned forward and spoke softly—"tell me . . . you call the white-haired lady Mamselle. She is not your mother then?"

"Oh, no. Mamselle is not married. I am an

orphan. I have been ever since I was four. Do you realize, Alouette, how nice it is to have a family . . . a big family with children around?"

"Oh, yes, but sometimes the little ones keep things pretty lively." Then she had a happy thought. "Do you know what? We are close neighbors and we can be best friends, and then you can share my family. What do you think of that?"

"I think it sounds wonderful!" Maria's eyes were sparkling. Then Alouette saw the light go out of her smile.

"Something is wrong?"

"Everything is wrong, Alouette."

"Tell me about it. If we are going to be best friends we ought to tell each other our troubles."

"Well . . . I don't know exactly where to begin. I guess money right now is the thing that is troubling Mamselle and Nana."

"Nana? The . . . uh . . . well, I guess I might as well tell you. I think Nana is pretty crotchety. I have been calling her the sour-faced one," Alouette confessed.

"Oh, Nana is crotchety all right. But Mamselle loves her, and she has taken care of Mamselle all her life. Nana has rheumatism. That's what makes her so cross. Mamselle and I pay no mind.

96

We just let her boss us around as she pleases. We know she has a heart of gold."

"In what way a heart of gold?"

"Well, Nana saved some money in Scotland many years ago. In fact, that is all we have had to live on. Now the money is running out and that is why I said everything is wrong. You see, we can't even afford to go on living here. We will have to move to just about the smallest and cheapest place we can find."

"But Mamselle?"

"Mamselle has never been herself since the accident. She remembers nothing that happened before the shipwreck on the way to Scotland. You see, she has what the doctors call amnesia. They say a shock, even a small one, might restore her memory, but it has been so long we are not very hopeful of ever making Mamselle remember anything that happened before that awful storm at sea."

Alouette's heart was knocking against her ribs like a triphammer. "So she really is the white-haired Mamselle?"

"Yes, but she doesn't even remember being called that. And please, Alouette, remember this. Mamselle is all right in every other way. It is just that, as the doctors say, her mind has blocked out the past."

"How did you and the Mamselle and Nana happen to be saved when the ship went down?"

"Oh, that! Well, Mamselle saved my life. I was four years old. I was born in Interlaken, Switzerland, but my father and mother and I had been to America. They lost their lives, and I have no other relatives."

"And the Mamselle?"

"Oh, that is the sad part of it. She risked her life saving mine. She had seen me on the ship with my parents and knew our stateroom was on the deck below hers. She went down when no one else had the courage to go, and rescued me. Somehow we got into a lifeboat, just the three of us. We drifted for days and finally, half starved and almost dying of thirst, we were picked up by a Scottish fishing boat.

"Mamselle was unconscious when we were rescued, and when she came to, her memory was gone. After that, Nana took us back to Scotland to a famous doctor. But he wasn't able to help her memory, even though he tried for years, so he finally told us to bring her back here. He thought it might restore her memory if she could recognize even a small thing that happened in the past. He said this was her only chance."

Tears were rolling down Alouette's cheeks now. "But it didn't restore her memory to bring her back."

"No, not even when Nana brought her a beautiful white horse and named it Colette after the one she had loved so much, and driven on the Island when she was a young girl."

"And the sleigh with the golden swans? Nana bought that too?"

"Oh, no. Would you believe it? All these years Mamselle's beautiful sleigh had been in storage in Quebec. It is as good as new, just as her father bought it for her when she was young."

"So the sleigh is the same?"

"Yes, and Mamselle loves this Colette dearly, but she does not remember that she had the first one."

Footsteps came toward them from the back of the house now.

"Well!" a grumbly voice interrupted them. "Of all the chatter I ever heard. You two sound like a couple of magpies. What foolishness could you find to talk about so soon?"

It was the old nurse, coming into the room, com-

99

plaining as usual. In her hands Nana was carrying a beautiful silver tea tray. She set it on a round table in front of the fireplace.

"And where is her ladyship, I should like to know. Dawdling while her tea is getting cold?"

"Here, Nana, right here," and the white-haired Mamselle came swiftly down the left side of the double staircase, her hand on the marble railing. She was dressed in white, her white hair piled high atop her head. "How do you do, my dear? It is wonderful to see you again," she said, putting her arm about Alouette's shoulder.

"She really is the Snow Queen," Alouette thought.

"It is about time you got here," said Nana grumpily. "I, for one, am ready for my tea. What kept you so long?"

"And you shall have your tea," the white-haired lady said smiling. "The very first cup." And Alouette was glad to see that instead of tea, Mamselle was pouring hot chocolate out of the silver pot.

"Take this to Nana, Maria," she said smiling, and handed the little girl the delicate porcelain cup of delicious-looking chocolate and a dainty napkin.

Maria carefully took the cup to Nana, who sat

in a big chair beside the fireplace. The old nurse nodded her thanks.

And now Alouette was watching the Mamselle serve the chocolate. Her hands fluttered over the table like white butterflies. On the third finger of her left hand she wore the cat's eye ring with flashing emeralds, the mate to the ring the Northern Traveler had given Alouette.

"Mamselle," Alouette said finally, leaning forward, "you have a beautiful ring."

"Yes, it is a beautiful ring." Mamselle's eyes seemed to have a puzzled look in them as she gazed silently at the ring.

Then the subject was changed. "And now another cup of chocolate around," Mamselle said brightly, and once again her lovely hands fluttered over the tea table.

And so the pleasant afternoon wore on, and no one realized it was nearing time for the happy occasion to end. No one, that is, but Nana, who rose and went hobbling out of the room to the back of the house. "Chatter, chatter, chatter," she complained.

"Does . . . does . . . your ring have a name in it, Mamselle?" Alouette asked. She felt as if she had to know whether the white-haired lady's ring bore the name "Mizpah" which she had found in her own ring.

"A name? A name? Why no, Alouette, there is no name in my ring. What an odd question. Whatever made you think it had a name in it?" Mamselle looked at her in surprise.

Alouette blushed to the roots of her taffy-colored hair.

"Well . . . oh . . . I . . . oh, it is five o'clock. I must be going." She glanced gratefully up at the grandfather clock on the stair landing as it boomed out the hour of five. Once again she felt that the old clock had taken a personal interest in her. It certainly had saved her from an embarrassing situation. Why indeed should she ask if the Mamselle's ring had a name in it?

"It has been a lovely tea," she said, putting on her red coat and kid mittens. "Maria, will you come to see me soon?"

"Of course I'll come. We are going to be best friends, you know."

"My goodness, it's getting dark," Alouette said as she stepped to the veranda and put on her boots.

Herbert and the sledge were waiting at the foot of the steps, and as Alouette went bumping down the avenue of trees Maria and the white-haired

102

Mamselle stood waving until she turned into the white road which is the King's Highway.

"It is as dark out here as the inside of my pocket," she said to Herbert. "But we are right at the farm gate, I can see. . . ."

She stopped talking to Herbert, for he had shied just beside the gate to the lane.

"Herbert! What is it?" She tried to see in the darkness what had made the horse shy.

Now a figure loomed at her elbow, a figure on snowshoes.

"How," said a familiar voice.

"How," said Alouette. "Where did you come from?"

"I am one who come from all over."

"What do you mean by that?"

"The Northern Traveler know what happen. He keep watch."

"What do you mean you keep watch?"

"I keep watch. I know you go to Lonesome Manor."

"I was there for tea."

"The white-haired one there, and ugly old one also?"

"Oh, yes, but she is only cranky because of rheumatism."

The Northern Traveler ignored this explanation. "Tell me," he said, stepping closer, "does white-haired one wear ring? Cat's eye ring?"

"Yes, like the one you gave me on a chain. Only here is a strange thing. The lady's ring does not have a name in it as mine has."

"Your ring have no name in it."

Alouette stared at him in open-mouthed amazement. "But . . ."

The Northern Traveler interrupted her. "Lady plan to stay Lonesome Manor?"

"No, there is no money left. The nurse has a little, not enough to keep the Manor. It is very sad."

"Did lady speak of voyage and shipwreck?"

"No. The little girl told me about that. The white-haired Mamselle saved her life. She is an orphan, the little girl. Her name is Maria."

"She not married then, white-haired Mamselle?"

"But why are you asking me all these questions?" Alouette said. "Do you know her, the Mamselle?"

The Northern Traveler shook his head. "Know her? No. Someone . . ."

He did not finish what he started to say.

"I go now on journey, long journey, but I return. Northern Traveler always return. Listen well. On first day of Christmas market, I return. Be there that day, when your grandfather go to market to set up trees. This two weeks before *fête* of little Jesus. At market you hear owl hoot three times. Listen carefully, for owl hoot again. I be waiting for you. I will have something great value for you when I come back."

And then, just as he had the first time, the mysterious Northern Traveler vanished into the whirling snowstorm. Alouette tried to see him through the veil of snow, but it was no use.

She turned Herbert and the old sledge into the lane just as the rim of night fell silently over the white world.

CHAPTER 8

Bad News

THE DAYS were magic now in the snow-covered world of French Canada. All the evergreens around the old farmhouse took on the look of Christmas trees as they stood mantled in white.

The Snow Man came earlier now because the children of the village walked to the small wooden schoolhouse on snowshoes. It was much easier to walk on the cleared road.

It was the custom these days for Grandmère to send Alouette down the lane, as soon as they heard the Snow Man's shovel, to invite him in for coffee.

Today, as Alouette waited for him, the red shawl held tightly over her head, she was thinking of a very exciting event.

"A tea party," she said to Armand, who stood beside her. "Imagine me giving a tea party this very afternoon at four." Armand wagged his tail in sympathetic delight.

"Here is the Snow Man," she exclaimed as the familiar blue sledge came to a halt.

"Grandmère says to come in for coffee."

"Certainly, I can smell it way out here in the road. If anything smells better on a cold day than hot coffee, it has not been invented on this earth," Edmond exclaimed, following her up the lane.

Then, with a great stamping of feet on the stoop, and his woolen cap in his hand, the genial Snow Man followed her into the warm, cozy kitchen-parlor. Here the huge coffeepot was steaming on the big stove, filling the air with cheer.

Edmond's black moustache bristled with anticipation. Alouette handed him the fragrant cup and with it, on a plate, a slice of homemade bread still warm from the oven, spread with sweet butter and blueberry jam.

"Well, Edmond," Maman said, pouring more coffee, "what is the news today?"

"Ah, well you may ask, Madame Robinette. The news is very bad today."

The Snow Man took a sip of coffee and turned

108

to Alouette. "As you well know by this time, I was mistaken, as was everyone else on the Island, in believing the white-haired Mamselle had been lost at sea."

Alouette nodded. "I told you . . ."

"Hush, Alouette, let the Snow Man speak," Maman said.

"Well, it seems the white-haired Mamselle's home, the Manor house, is to be sold at once. The old Scottish nurse's money is running out. They have no one to turn to."

"It seems such a pity," Grandmère said. "The white-haired Mamselle has always been so kind and thoughtful."

"Yes, the white-haired Mamselle is a lady born and bred. She has always been kind to everyone. And here, then, is her reward. She cannot even keep her own roof over her head and the heads of those she loves."

"It's almost time for school," Alouette said, looking at the clock, "but before I go down the lane I have news for you."

"Well, I could use a little news, something besides new babies. Twins at the Chevalls."

"How many does that make?" Grandmère asked.

"Fourteen or perhaps more. I doubt if the Chevalls themselves know," Edmond replied, setting down his cup.

"Well, my news has nothing to do with babies," Alouette said. "This is real news."

"Good news, I hope?"

"The best. I am having a tea party as soon as I get home from school this afternoon."

"This is amazing," exclaimed the Snow Man.

"Yes, and a very stylish party. Maria, the little girl from the Manor is coming here to take tea with us."

"Only the tea will be chocolate, and Grandmère is going to make a torte this high," Chichi put in.

"This is remarkable," the Snow Man said. "I could stand here listening all day, but I am an important government official and I must keep King's Highway cleared or you little ones cannot get to school. The coffee was delicious, and I thank you, Madame Robinette."

"Oh, dear, there's the school bell now," Alouette said as the Snow Man went out. André stood in the lane.

"Hurry and get your snowshoes on," Alouette called to her brother in the lane. "André, hurry! The school bell is ringing."

110

"Who knows that better than I do, and I'll soon have my snowshoes on."

"Maman's dressing the little ones. Wait until I kiss them goodby, and I'll be with you in the lane."

Alouette rushed to the room where the baby and the twins were being dressed, and kissed each of them. Then she ran out to the side door and joined André after she had buckled on her own snowshoes. Lifting their feet and setting them down, which is the way to walk on snowshoes, they went toward the schoolhouse whose somewhat cracked bell filled the winter air with a jangling melody of its own.

As the day wore on, it was very hard for Alouette to keep her mind on her lessons. Her thoughts strayed too often to the preparations for the tea party for the little girl who was coming from the Manor.

But at last the clock in the schoolroom pointed to three, and school was dismissed. Alouette hastened into her coat and went slipping and sliding, for the road was getting icy. Finally she and André reached the comfortable warmth of the old farmhouse.

"Are you going to help Papa and Grandpère this afternoon?" Alouette asked, as they thrust their snowshoes upright in the drifted snow beside the door.

"No!"

"What are you going to do then?"

"Go out in the barn and talk to Herbert."

"But the tea party!"

"Pooh! You couldn't make me come to that old party. Have you gone out of your mind? Who wants to go to a party with girls?"

"All right." There was a slight note of relief in his sister's voice that André did not notice as they stepped inside.

The kitchen-parlor had never seemed so friendly and warm and inviting, but Alouette flew into a frenzy of activity at once.

"Why must I put on my Sunday dress?" Chichi wanted to know, as her sister thrust her into her best outfit.

"Because, my angel, this little girl is used to very stylish things."

"Am I stylish?" Chichi asked.

"Oh, very, very stylish. And Maman is going to leave the baby in her cradle in her room, and the twins will be taking their naps. It is going to be a very stylish tea party."

"Aren't babies stylish, Alouette?" Chichi asked.

Alouette laughed and hugged her little sister. "Babies are the most stylish things in French Canada, my little one. It's just their nap time, and Maman and Grandmère thought it would be nice for you and Maria and me to take tea at a little table alone. I asked André, but he said he'd rather stay in the barn and talk to Herbert."

"What will he and Herbert talk about?"

"Who knows?" Alouette gave her small sister a pat on the back of her starched pinafore. "There you are, Chichi. You look beautiful with a blue bow in your hair and a blue dress. You are the beauty of the Robinette family."

"I know," Chichi said with confidence. "I know, because Grandpère tells me I'm the most beautiful girl on the Island of Orléans, all of French Canada, and maybe the whole world even."

"Well, Grandpère is taking in a lot of territory," Alouette said, smoothing her own starched pinafore down for the seventh time.

On the stroke of four, sleigh bells were heard out on the road. Alouette pressed her nose flat against the window. The white sleigh was just turning in the gate.

"Isn't it wonderful, here she comes!" she cried, and ran out the door to welcome her guest who had been driven by the silent old caretaker of Lonesome Manor.

"Oh, I never saw anything so lovely as this room," Maria cried as she came into the kitchen-parlor where a bright fire was crackling on the hearth. A small table drawn up in front of it was set with Maman's best china.

"And I never saw anything so lovely as your white fur coat and hat," said Alouette, taking her guest's coat politely. "And . . . I didn't even know they made white shoes."

The little girl laughed, but she made a remark that did not sound very happy. "Well, anyway," she said, "when I outgrow these white shoes I will be lucky if I can have black ones."

Maman and Grandmère came in then and Alouette introduced them to her new friend.

"Oh, and this is Chichi, my little sister."

"Chichi! Oh, yes, Alouette told us all about you the day she was down at the Manor," said Maria.

"She did? Did she tell you how stylish I am?" Chichi asked with interest.

"Yes, she told me that, too."

And then Maman came in with piping hot chocolate, served in her dearest possession, the silver

114

chocolate pot that had been in her family for generations. The chocolate pot had over it a pink tea cozy to keep it warm, but Alouette knew the gleaming pot was underneath.

Then Grandmère brought in the beautiful torte, cut and ready for Alouette to serve with the chocolate, and after that there was no one in the room but three chattering little girls, the farm dog, and Minou with her kittens.

"Oh, I dearly love kittens," cried Maria. "Do you know where I could buy one?"

"Buy one? Buy a kitten?" Alouette thought her ears were playing tricks on her. "Who ever heard of buying a kitten?"

"How do you get them then?" Maria wanted to know.

"Why, they just come naturally, I guess. Anyhow, this one, Minou, has kittens and kittens and kittens. I'm always trying to find homes for kittens. I spend a lot of time doing this. They must have *good* homes. The very best."

"I'd give them a good home, Alouette. I'd like to have both of them when they are older. I may not be able to give them a home in the Manor, but we will be somewhere on the Island . . . somewhere in a little house. Mamselle seems better here than

115

any place, and Nana wants to stay even if we have to give up the Manor. I guess the old house was just intended to be Lonesome Manor."

Alouette put her hand on Maria's. "I . . . I wish you could keep the Manor. It really is so very beautiful."

Maria nodded. "Yes, the Manor is beautiful, but the hardest thing to part with is Colette."

"No! Not the white horse!" Alouette was so startled she barely missed upsetting Mama's silver chocolate pot.

"Yes, Colette and the white sleigh both. Nana has not told Mamselle this yet. She is afraid it will break her heart. But there is just not enough money."

Alouette sat helpless and aghast as two big tears rolled down Maria's cheeks. Then she changed the subject and began to chatter about school, but not for long, for a surprising thing happened.

The back door flew open and André scuttled up the stairs. In a very little while he was down again, standing between his sisters.

"My heavens," Alouette thought, "he has washed his face and combed his hair. And . . . and he has put on a clean blue shirt. This I can't believe."

116

But she did not put her thoughts into words. Instead she said very politely, "Maria, this is my brother André."

Maria looked up at him and smiled. "How do you do, André? I am happy to meet you."

And André, blushing furiously, grinned sheepishly and bobbed his sleekly combed head.

"Will you have some chocolate and a piece of torte?" Alouette asked in her most polite hostess manner.

André shook his head. "No, thank you," he replied.

"Now I've heard everything," Alouette thought.

117

But she had not heard everything, for Chichi was smiling and chattering to Maria, and what she said almost made her older brother and sister sink through the floor.

"Do you know what?" said Chichi, much pleased with herself. "André said he'd rather stay out in the barn and talk to the horse than take tea with girls."

"Oh, Chichi, hush!" Alouette exclaimed, but the bewildered little girl looked anxiously into her brother's blazing face.

"You sick or something?" she asked.

Everyone had to laugh then, and Alouette said, "You see how it is to have a family, Maria?"

"Just the same, I'd love it. I'd like to have a father and a mother. You see, Mamselle is the same as a mother, but she can't really adopt me without getting married. It's against the law or something. Single ladies can't adopt children."

After this there was quiet in the room and only the fire broke the silence.

Then there was a shower of melody in the road, and the white sleigh drawn by Colette stopped at the door.

"It's been the most wonderful party I ever went to," Maria said to Grandmère and Alouette.

118

And then, to Alouette's amazement, André opened the door for Maria and helped her into the sleigh.

"Now I have seen *everything*," Alouette said as André came back into the house.

André gave his sister a sheepish grin. "Is there any chocolate and torte left?" he asked.

"Of course." Alouette sighed with relief. André was acting himself again.

After she went to bed that night, Alouette thought over the things that had been spoken of that day.

The Snow Man had said the Mamselle would have to give up the Manor. That had been bad enough. But when Maria said the beautiful white horse must go also . . . the lovely Colette . . . "Why, that will break Mamselle's heart," she said aloud. "If there was only something I could do to help them!"

But what could a little farm girl do to save the beloved pet for the white-haired Mamselle?

It seemed there was no possible answer to these questions. Alouette pulled back her curtain and looked down the snow-covered road that led to the old house . . . the house that was soon again to become Lonesome Manor.

CHAPTER **9**

The Christmas Market

WINTER HAD deepened now, and Christmas hovered in the air. The little wood school with the round stove was closed to give the children a chance to prepare for the *fête* of the little Jesus.

Alouette and Maria had become the best of friends, and were busily making their plans for Christmas together.

On one very snowy afternoon Maman and Grandmère set out to call on the white-haired Mamselle, dressed in their best Sunday clothes, with Maman driving Herbert hitched to the old farm sledge.

Alouette could hardly wait until they came

home, and was watching at the frosty window when the sledge turned up the lane.

"How was she? How was it? Did you take tea, or what then?" She began firing questions so fast that Maman shook her head.

"First things first," she said, removing her woolen scarf.

"Yes, the white-haired Mamselle was very nice to us, and we did take tea. She is a very gracious lady."

"Did she say anything about selling the Manor, or selling Colette?" Alouette wanted to know.

"Yes, but she said no one seemed to want the Manor as it is too expensive to keep up. Mamselle did not mention the white horse, but she is very sad . . . and she did not recognize us from the past when we were friends. She only knew us as the Robinettes, your grandmother and mother." Maman shook her head. "It is a great pity, her memories of the past are gone entirely.

"I even spoke of Cousin Jacques Robinette, to whom she had been betrothed . . . just mentioned, mind you, that he had been my cousin, but it brought no recollection at all, even when I said he had gone astray."

"What did she say?" Alouette wanted to know.

"She just said it was very tragic when someone went astray in the bitter winter forest.

"And now," Maman said, "I must see about supper. Grandpère and Papa are in the wood lot cutting down the Christmas trees."

"Cutting down the trees today?" Alouette said. "How can that be happening so soon?"

"It is not so soon," her mother said. "The *fête* of the little Jesus is just around the corner . . . only two weeks away. They are taking the trees to the Christmas market in the morning."

"My gracious," Alouette muttered, remembering the Northern Traveler's instructions to be at the Christmas market the first day. He had told her to listen for the sound of a hoot owl calling three times, then three times again, and she was to follow the sound and he would have something of value for her. But to think it was the season for the Christmas market already . . . where had the time gone?

Alouette slept fitfully that night and was up and dressed before anyone in the family.

The Snow Man came in as usual for his coffee and gossip.

"I hear that the sour-faced one has found a purchaser for the white horse," he informed her.

"Oh, no, it can't be," Alouette said. "It just can't be!"

"Well, it won't be until the *fête* of the little Jesus is over. No binding bargain has been struck. And they say also that the Mamselle has been advised to have the old Manor house torn down and to sell the land. It is surrounded by fine farmland, but no one wants the house. It costs too much to keep a house like that going."

Alouette stood speechless for once in her life, as the Snow Man departed to conduct his important business as a government official.

Now breakfast was over, and Grandpère said, "I should like to have company at the Christmas market today. Papa and André are still cutting down Christmas trees."

"I'll go and keep you company," said Chichi in her small piping voice.

Grandpère patted her fair head and said, "Next year, my little one. This year you are just too young. I think Alouette is the best one to take this year."

"Oh, yes please." Alouette's heart was knocking against her ribs. Suppose she had not been permitted to go. What then?

But she *was* going, and now she and Grandpère

were seated on the big sledge which had been piled high with pungent Christmas trees.

Over the long road they went, a bearskin robe over their knees, and Herbert's harness bell tinkling out a tune that sounded very much like a Christmas carol. Through the town of Levis they went, over the great bridge that spans the St. Lawrence River, past the lovely ancient church, Notre Dame des Victoires, and on into Quebec. In the center of the old town stood the Christmas market.

It was here that the French Canadian farmers brought their beautiful Christmas trees to stand upright in the snow and form the fragrant forest of evergreens called the Christmas market.

Alouette worked to help Grandpère set up his trees in his reserved space. When the task was finished, her grandfather went to visit with a group of old friends.

"So the Northern Traveler didn't keep his word," Alouette was thinking. There was no sign of the mysterious man in the market . . . no sound of an owl hooting. She sat down on the sledge to watch the people selecting their Christmas trees.

Alouette and her grandfather had lunch in a small restaurant nearby, and the day wore on. Still there was no sign of the Northern Traveler.

125

Then, as they were packing up to return to the Island of Orléans, Alouette heard the sound she had been waiting for all day . . . the hooting of an owl. *"One, two, three,"* she counted, then *"one, two, three,"* again. She walked toward the sound as Grandpère was busily engaged in making a last-minute sale.

Slowly, so that she would not attract attention, she walked toward the insistent and soft call of the owl. Then she stopped. Something moved a little behind a large, bushy Christmas tree, and Alouette saw that it was a hand beckoning.

She walked toward the beckoning hand.

"Here!" said a quiet voice, a voice from behind the Christmas tree.

"How." Alouette gave the greeting of the upraised hand as she came face to face with the Northern Traveler.

"I have only short time," he whispered. "This night I start on long, long journey to far North."

"Not another journey on snowshoes?" Alouette gasped, remembering what her grandmother had told her about her Cousin Jacques going astray.

The Northern Traveler shook his head. "Do not fear for me. There other ways to go north. I not always go on snowshoes.

"But enough this talk. Here small gift for you,
but you must take much care." He placed the gift
in her mittened hand, and Alouette stared down
at it.

"Oh, it's a little clock, a little clock against a
carved panel. It's exactly like the clock and panel
at the head of the stairs in Lonesome Manor.
Where in the world did it come from?"

"From Lonesome Manor," was the Indian's surprising answer.

"But how did you come by it?"

The Traveler heaved a deep sigh. "I sorry to tell you I had ancestor among bad Indians who attack Manor day old Laird carried off. I not proud of this bad ancestor. I spend my life trying help people your race to make up for sins mine.

"Take little clock home in pocket. It carry a secret. But what secret be, I not know. Show clock no one but little girl at Lonesome Manor."

"Why not the white-haired Mamselle and the old nurse?"

"No! I must have your promise. It be too sad if nothing come this. We must not make white-haired one worry more. If little clock do what you want it do, then will be time enough tell Mamselle."

"But . . . what . . . what is the secret?"

"You find for yourself. I not know, and my people before me not know. It kept hidden away for over hundred years. Only now I find by chance."

For the first time the Northern Traveler smiled. "My ancestors think clock instrument of evil. They tell time of day by sun."

"Why didn't they destroy the clock then, instead of hiding it away?"

"They afraid. They afraid little clock have devilish powers that bewitch!"

As Alouette slipped the little clock into her coat pocket, she wondered how she could solve the mystery of Lonesome Manor with a toy clock.

The Northern Traveler looked at her steadily. "You solve it. It written in stars. I go now, but you hear owl hooting again in week. It be early in morning, outside your gate. Be there when owl hoot, for I will have such surprise for you as no one on Island ever dream." And with these words, he turned away and vanished among the groves of Christmas trees in the old market place.

All the way home, and even through supper, Alouette was very quiet.

"Has the cat got your tongue?" Chichi asked.

"No, I was thinking."

"What about?"

"Chichi, you don't have to know everything," Maman said, coming to Alouette's defense.

But it was not until bedtime that Alouette could remove the little clock from her pocket. She set it under the lamp on the washstand. For a long while she studied it.

"It is exactly like the big friendly grandfather clock that stands on the landing at Lonesome

Manor," she thought. "Here is the pointed carved panel, and everything is the same except I don't remember seeing the two carved roses on either side of the clock. But I wasn't close enough to see. . . . The carved roses . . . I wonder . . ."

She gave the rose on the right-hand side of the panel a twist, but the rose did not budge from its original position. She repeated the performance on the left-hand side, and still nothing happened.

"All right, so you are keeping your secret, eh?" she said. "Pooh!" And she gave the right-hand rose an impatient poke with her forefinger.

Instantly the carved wooden panel swung open, carrying the clock with it. And as this happened, a lively tune tinkled from the little clock.

Alouette stared down at the tinkling music box in amazement.

"What is that tune? Oh, yes, I know. It's that old nursery rhyme:

'Hickory, dickory, dock,
The mouse ran up the clock.'

I wonder what this silly little toy has to do with the secret of Lonesome Manor?"

She closed the panel and the music stopped. Then she pressed the carved rose on the right side,

130

as she had done before, and again the old nursery song tinkled forth.

Alouette had been so surprised that the clock had turned out to be a music box that she had not examined the inside of the panel. Now she peered into it curiously.

"Why, something is moving in there!" She looked again. "It's . . . oh no! . . . it can't be, but it is! It's a toy mouse and it's climbing, it's climbing a little circular stairway in the panel."

Alouette sat down. "So that's it. That must be the secret. There's a spiral stairway, I'll bet, back of the panel behind the big grandfather clock on the landing. Now if the big clock has roses on either side of it, and the right one works, this could be the entrance to the windowless tower. The secret entrance!"

But how could she get into Lonesome Manor without the old one and Mamselle knowing? The Northern Traveler had said no one but Maria must be told about the clock until she had some proof that it was the key to the mystery.

"Alouette?" It was André outside her door. "I thought I heard music. It sounds like a little music box playing. Do you hear it?"

Alouette closed the panel quickly and stuffed

131

the little clock under her pillow. "Go back to bed," she said.

"But don't you hear?"

"Go back to bed. I hear nothing but the snow tapping at the windowpane," she said quite truthfully.

CHAPTER **10**

The Old Clock on the Landing

"ALOUETTE." It was the piping voice of Chichi outside her door. "Maman says to get up. We're having ham and shambled eggs for breakfast."

"Shambled eggs? What an idea. Come in then."

Chichi came in, holding something behind her. "Guess what I've got?"

"A new kitten, maybe?"

"No, it's a note! The old caretaker from the Manor brought it early this morning. It's for you."

"Well, give it to me then."

Chichi brought the note from its hiding place and handed it to her sister. "What does it say?"

"How would I know until I read it?"

Alouette opened the note and read:

Dear Alouette:

Mamselle and Nana are going to Quebec on business. Mamselle says I must stay home because I have a light case of sniffles. She says she would be happy if you could come and stay with me. They are leaving about ten this morning. Nana has made sandwiches, and there are cookies and milk, so we won't starve.

The note was signed "Your best friend, Maria."

"Well then—" she looked at Chichi— "tell Maman I'll be right down for the ham and shambled eggs. What a wonderful day this will be!" Alouette exclaimed as she flew into a whirlwind of activity. Shambled eggs for breakfast, and a chance to show Maria the little music box clock and see if it really was the key to the mystery of Lonesome Manor.

It was shortly before ten when Alouette drove the big sledge bumping down King's Highway toward the Manor.

"Saints alive," Alouette complained to Herbert. "The rougher this road gets, the faster you go. Who can sit still with all this bouncing? Oh well, I might as well be happy. At least I don't have to

134

go on snowshoes. It's slippery as glass this morning." As usual, she began to whistle.

"There she goes," croaked the nosy Madame Durand, peeping through her window. "I tell you, a whistling girl and a crowing hen . . ."

"I know, I know," her husband said, holding up an impatient hand, and finishing the saying, ". . . always come to some bad end."

"Well, so you have come to my way of thinking then," his wife said triumphantly.

Her spouse shook his head. "Not by any manner of means. I believe that that little whistling one out there in the snow will have a happy future."

But Monsieur Durand had no idea exactly what this good fortune might be.

Alouette arrived at the Manor just as the white-haired Mamselle and Nana pulled through the iron gateway with Colette and the white-and-gold sleigh. She waved a cheery hand, and they waved back to her as they drove over the road toward Quebec.

Alouette turned into the driveway, bouncing high and coming down with a thump on the hard wooden seat as Herbert came to a sudden stop at the front steps of the veranda. The silent care-

135

taker took charge of Herbert as Alouette mounted the stone steps.

"Come in quickly." Maria poked her head out the door.

"Go back inside. You'll catch more cold," Alouette said, hurrying through the door and closing it.

"Maria, I have a secret, a secret you wouldn't believe. A secret just for you and me."

Breathlessly Alouette took off her red coat and reached into the pocket, producing the toy clock.

"What is it? What is the secret? Tell me."

"Wait till I show you." Alouette pushed the tiny rose-carved knob, the panel flew open and the strains of the ancient nursery tune tinkled through the quiet old Manor.

"Why, why I used to hear that in Switzerland when I was very little. Almost everyone in Switzerland has a music box. It is called the land of music boxes. Where did you get the little clock?"

"Wait till I tell you. Such a business!"

Then Alouette told the round-eyed Maria the story of the Northern Traveler and the Christmas market.

"Does the little clock look familiar to you?" Alouette asked when she had finished the story.

Maria shook her head.

"For goodness sakes! Look up the stairway in this very hall."

Maria raised her eyes to the stair landing. "Oh . . . it's exactly like the big clock there on the landing."

"And what do you think of this?" Alouette pointed to the spiral stairway hidden in the panel of the toy clock, with the toy mouse ascending it. "Do you know what that means?"

"It means a toy mouse is climbing a spiral stairway. That's all I can see."

"Well—" Alouette took a deep breath— "I think it means that the hidden stairway to the secret tower in the Manor is behind the clock and panel up there."

"The windowless tower? The stairway is behind the clock?"

Alouette nodded. "Only one thing. I . . . can't . . . see the knobs on the panel beside the big clock. Let's go up and look at it on the landing."

Lickety-split, the two girls ran up the curving marble stairs.

Alouette stood facing the big clock which chose that very moment to boom out the half hour.

"My goodness! It almost scared me to death

when it boomed at me like that." Alouette's pig-tails were bristling with excitement. She ran her fingers over the left-hand side of the carved panel. Maria stood holding the music box with wide, excited eyes.

"Yes . . . I've found the knob. It is here, carved in the wood. Just like the little one . . . a carved wooden rose."

Alouette pressed the left-hand rose but nothing happened.

"Oh . . . no . . . no . . . it is the right-hand knob." She wiped her perspiring hands on her pinafore. "Now here I go. If nothing happens I will know the clock is only a toy with no other meaning."

She took a long, deep breath and pushed. At first nothing happened, then slowly, with a moaning, creaking sound, the old panel began to open. Slowly it swung outward, its creaking hinges complaining and echoing in the big hall.

"Look . . . look, Alouette, the clock is fastened to the panel. It's swinging out with it, just like the music box." Maria was hopping excitedly from one foot to the other.

But Alouette was staring into the darkness behind the clock.

"I can't see what is back there until I get my

night eyes," she whispered, "but I think I see a stairway . . . a winding, spiral stairway. But no mouse."

Once again she took a deep breath. Then she turned and faced Maria. "I'm going up the spiral stairway to the secret tower."

"I'll go with you," Maria said in a small, timid voice.

"No! You will catch more cold. There is a draft coming down the stairs."

Alouette did not want to tell her friend the thought going around in her head, "Who knows what might be up there?"

She examined the inside of the door. "The knob works on the inside, too, so if the door closes it won't be locked," she told Maria.

And so, as the speechless Maria watched, Alouette mounted the narrow and winding stairs. Round and round they went, for they were steep and dark. At the head of the stairs, she was met with a startling surprise. A figure was standing beside the entrance to the windowless tower.

Alouette peered through the gloom. "Who . . . who . . . are . . . you . . . ?" she asked in a shaky voice. The figure did not speak or move.

Alouette went closer, then began to laugh. The

figure standing in the gloomy old tower was a suit of armor.

"So you have been guarding this tower all these years," she said aloud.

Way down below, at the foot of the stairs, a small voice called to her, "Whom are you talking to, Alouette?"

"An old suit of armor," Alouette called back. Then she began looking about her. There was nothing in the tower except three iron benches. It was true the tower was without windows, but there were three small openings in the stone wall

140

through which a few feeble rays of light sifted. The cold air that blew in from the St. Lawrence River made her shiver.

"Nothing. There is nothing up here that anyone would want." Alouette stamped her foot. "And you," she said to the metal suit of armor, "you, standing here all these years doing nothing!" She gave the figure an angry push.

The figure tottered a moment. Then, with a tremendous crash, the heavy metal suit of armor fell to the floor. Alouette, peering through the gloom, saw its head rolling and bouncing down the spiral staircase.

She ran down the stairs herself then, but not before the bodyless head had landed at the very feet of the horrified Maria.

"Don't worry," Alouette called, "it's only the helmet of a suit of rusty old armor.

"Let's pick it up and see what it really looks like," she said, closing the panel back of the clock. But to her amazement, the head of the armored figure was so heavy it took all of her own and Maria's strength combined to lift it to the table that stood on the landing.

"Look, it's partly open, here at the visor." Maria touched the opening with a cautious finger. "I

141

have seen lots of armor like this in old castles in Europe."

"Here . . ." Alouette wrested the visor farther apart and thrust her hand inside. "Let me see now." She rolled her eyes. "There is something in it," she said. "Look! It is very heavy—it's a bag made out of some sort of animal hide."

Alouette lifted the bag from the helmet and untied the leather thongs. Then she peered in, and gasped. "Goodness gracious! What do you think this is?"

She held out something round and shining in her hand.

"It . . . it looks like a gold piece," Maria said.

"It *is* a gold piece. My goodness! This bag is full of gold coins. Maria, there *was* a treasure hidden in that old tower, and we have found it! Do you know what this means then?"

Maria shook her head. "I didn't find it. You did."

"It means that Mamselle will not have to part with Colette, and that you can all stay in the Manor forever. Oh, dear . . . here they come now, Mamselle and Nana."

Alouette ran to the door. "Hurry! Hurry!" she cried. "Please, Mamselle, come in at once."

142

"Just a moment, dear. Has something happened?"

"Yes, something good, something wonderful. We have found the hidden treasure in the tower. We have found the old Laird's gold."

"What kind of silly humbug is this?" Nana said crossly. "There is no treasure in the tower, and even if there were, there is no way to get up there. A lot of good it will do us."

"It's here . . . it's here on the landing. Cross my heart, this is not humbug. It is the truth. I wouldn't tease you about anything as important as this."

"Come on, Nana," said the white-haired Mamselle, smiling indulgently. "This may be a make-believe game but it won't hurt either of us to go up to the landing and pretend with them."

So, grumbling and mumbling, the old woman followed her mistress up the red-carpeted marble stairs, while Alouette ran ahead excitedly.

"They don't believe it," she said to Maria. "But they've *got* to believe it. It is the Mamselle's money!"

But they did believe her when Alouette put her hand inside the leather pouch and pulled it out tightly clutching a fistful of gold pieces.

143

"It's . . . it's real!" Nana gasped and suddenly sat down on a velvet bench. "I . . . I . . . had heard rumors that a treasure was hidden up there, but there is so much gossip and superstition on this Island that I could not really believe it was true."

"It *is* gold, my dear, lots of gold. But I don't understand—Alouette how did you come by it?" It was Mamselle speaking.

Then Alouette told her the story of the little musical clock and showed her how it worked. After this, she pushed the carved rose beside the big clock, and the white-haired Mamselle followed her up the narrow, spiral stairway to the secret tower above.

This time Maria went up, but nothing could induce the old Scottish nurse to mount the steep, narrow steps. "Not with my rheumatic knees. I'd never make it."

"You see, the armor fell when I pushed it," Alouette explained. "I was angry because he was just standing there doing nothing, and there was no treasure in sight. And then his head fell off and rolled all the way down the steps, and it almost frightened Maria to death. She thought it was a real head and . . ."

Alouette stopped chattering and peered through

144

the gloom. "There was something else in that helmet, something that fell out before it rolled down the stairs."

She went over and picked up a small book. The book was covered with a thick layer of dust, which she tried to blow off.

"This is yours, as well as the gold. They both belonged to your ancestors." She held the little book out toward the white-haired Mamselle.

"I . . . I . . . can't remember. I can't remember. If Nana says the gold belongs to me, I will take it, and the little book also. And you, Alouette, you will be the talk of Ste. Famille, and well-rewarded."

"No reward, Mamselle," Alouette said when they were down in the great hall again and she had closed the secret panel.

"Alouette says the gold belongs to me," the white-haired Mamselle said to the old nurse, who was poking the fire in the big fireplace.

"Of course it belongs to you. There are no other heirs. It was found in your house. It was hidden by your ancestors and found here." Nana turned around and looked squarely at Alouette. "And was found by a nosy little girl."

But Alouette smiled because Nana was laugh-

145

ing when she said it. She had never seen the sour-faced one smile before.

"And the little book?" Alouette said, blowing the dust off into the fireplace. "Are you not going to read the little book, Mamselle?"

"You read it," Mamselle said. "You read it aloud, and we will listen."

So Alouette opened the book. The pages were covered with words written in a fine, spidery hand. The ink was faded, and some of the words were blotched as if the writer had been weeping. "Well, all right . . ." Alouette began to read:

Tonight my children and I are leaving under cover of darkness. We are leaving the Island forever to return to Scotland. This new world is no place for a woman without her husband.

As is the custom of my country, my husband's younger brother, who is next in line, is the rightful heir to the Manor. Whether he will want to become the Laird of the Manor or not, I do not know. But I do want him to have certain information.

I am writing this for the new heir to read in case he does take up residence here. And I shall leave this book on the mantel in the

great hall, so that he and all the McPher-
sons who come later shall know how the
Manor house is built and why.

Here Alouette interrupted her reading. "She
forgot to bring it downstairs as she planned, the
poor lady."

Then Alouette continued to read:

The tower and its secret stairway were
built to protect the children from the savage Indians who roam this wild, new
country.

My husband employed a wood carver
and a famous clockmaker, who came from
Switzerland especially to fashion the carved
Gothic panel and the tall clock, to guard
the secret entrance to the stairway that
leads to the windowless tower.

As a special gift to the children, when
the big panel and clock were finished, these
two craftsmen made a small replica which
in every way represents the original. All,
that is, with the exception of the tiny mouse
that runs up the stairs when the panel is
opened, and the musical tune of "Hickory,
dickory, dock." These were put in solely
for the amusement of the little ones.

147

On the dreaded day when the Indians came at last, my husband saw them from the widow's walk of the small tower.

The Indians were landing in their birch-bark canoes at the edge of the St. Lawrence River, and soon were coming toward the Manor. They were in war paint and war regalia. It was a fearful sight.

My husband hastened down from the widow's walk and into the great hall to warn me to assemble the children and hide them in the secret tower at once.

And then a terrible thing happened. Aimé, our youngest, ran back for the little musical clock. I did not know she was not with us, and had it not been for her father's quick thinking she would have been captured, for a fierce Indian in war paint seized her by the arm. In so doing, Aimé's thumb struck the carved rose on the right-hand side of the little musical box and it began to play.

The sound of the music so astonished the Indian that he let go of the child's arm, and in that instant my husband picked Aimé up, pressed the carved rose in the panel behind the clock, and thrust Aimé into the secret stairway where she joined us in the tower.

It was this act that cost my husband his life. The Indian who had seized Aimé thrust the little clock in the front of his leather shirt to hide it from view. Indians, it seems, believe that clocks are instruments of evil. It was because of this superstition that my husband had conceived the idea of placing the big clock on the panel at the head of the stairs. I am sure the Indian who took the little clock saw the panel open, but he would not go near the big clock. He did, however, seize my husband.

Shivering with terror in the windowless tower, my children and I heard fierce animallike howling, and we knew the Indians were doing a victory dance.

Then all was silent and hours later, when we came down from the tower, my husband had disappeared and we have never seen him again.

So, after waiting here for two years, I am going back. I am leaving most of the fortune my husband made in this New World in the tower. It is too heavy for me to carry, because it is in gold. I am taking enough to pay our passage. The rest of it goes to the heir of the Manor. The gold is hidden in the ancient suit of armor in the windowless tower.

The key that opens the secret passage, as I have said before, is the carved rose on the right-hand side of the clock.

And so, tonight we are leaving. As darkness falls we shall go down the St. Lawrence River. It is not safe to travel by day.

I am leaving one last word for the one who finds this book. The people of French Canada have a saying, "Walk with God."

The letter was signed "Jean McPherson, May 21st. In the year of our Lord 17—" The rest of the date had been blotted out with tears.

Alouette placed the book in Mamselle's lap. Everyone in the quiet room was fighting valiantly to keep from weeping, even the crotchety old nurse.

"So, Mamselle," Alouette said, "you can see very well that the Laird's treasure belongs to you. You can keep Colette, and you are the real lady of the Manor. And, now, I hear Herbert's bell. The sledge is waiting for me at the steps."

"Alouette—" the white-haired Mamselle bent and kissed her—"I ... I ... can never, never thank you for what you have done."

"Oh, pooh! It was lots of fun to solve the mystery of Lonesome Manor." And with this casual remark, Alouette mounted the hard seat of the sledge and went bouncing and whistling down the long white road toward home. Finally she shook her head, and the red pompon atop her hood bobbed. "What a day!" she said to the back of Herbert's head.

CHAPTER **11**

The Owl Hoots Again

ALOUETTE unharnessed Herbert and gave him a pail of good sweet oats before she went into the house.

"I can't wait. I just can't wait to see André's face when I tell him of this day's doings," she thought. "I just can't wait."

It was a stroke of luck for her that the family was assembled in the kitchen-parlor for supper when she went in.

"Well, Featherhead, have you been taking tea again at the Manor ?" André asked. "And what kept you so long?"

"Pooh! And no, I have not been taking tea at the Manor."

"Chocolate, then?" Chichi asked. "Did you have little cakes and chocolate?"

"No, no chocolate, my angel." Alouette untied her hood and took her red coat and hung them up and took her place at the table.

"Well, what *have* you been doing?" André asked, looking at her curiously. "You'd better make it a good story."

"It is a good story. I've been discovering the hidden stairway that leads to the windowless tower and the old Laird's fortune, hidden in a suit of armor." Alouette tried as best she could to make the matter sound as if it were all in the day's work.

"A good story," André muttered. "But no one would believe it."

Alouette laid down her knife and fork. "Why not? It's the truth. Cross my heart, and you'll have proof tomorrow."

"Alouette, I believe you *are* telling the truth." Her brother looked at her in round-eyed astonishment. "The Laird's treasure!"

"Hush, André, let your sister tell us," her father said reprovingly. All eyes were fixed on Alouette now.

Alouette drew a long, deep breath. "Well then . . ." and the whole story of the day's doings

154

came tumbling out as fast as she could find the words.

Over and over the story was told and questions answered, as the evening wore on and night fell over the country.

"And the man's head went *boom, boom, boom,* right down the stairs," Chichi kept repeating.

"Not a real man's head, only armor," Alouette tried to explain, until finally Grandpère rose to his feet.

"You will be the heroine of the Island tomorrow, Alouette, but tonight you must scoot to bed. All of you."

But Alouette could not sleep. For a long time she lay listening to the floors of the old house creaking as the bitter night drew in.

"What was that?" It seemed she had only dozed off when a sound awakened her. It was an owl hooting, coming from the gateway in the lane. *"Whoo, whoo, whoo."*

Alouette leaped from her bed. She looked through her window, but all she could see were the pointing shadows the tall trees made on the snow.

"Whoo, whoo, whoo." There it was again.

Quick as a flash, she was into her robe and boots.

She flung the red shawl over her head and shoulders, and sped down the lane.

It was still dark, but the first faint rim of day was coming over the treetops.

A figure disengaged itself from the shadows and came forth with uplifted hand.

"How!"

It was the Northern Traveler. He had kept his word and returned.

Alouette returned his greeting, her teeth chattering.

"I have kept my word," said the Indian gravely. "I say you hear owl hoot at dawn, beside gate."

"Yes." Alouette was shivering with nerves and the cold.

"I said you," the Traveler continued, "I would have such surprise for you as no one in Ste. Famille ever dream."

Alouette nodded.

"Now, here is surprise."

The Northern Traveler stepped back, and a tall figure emerged from the deep shadow of the gatepost.

Alouette was afraid the tall stranger would hear her teeth rattling as he came toward her.

"This man . . . this, then, is the surprise?"

Alouette asked, and was happy at this moment to see the lamplight appear in the kitchen. "Grand-mère is up, thank goodness," she thought. She felt more courageous with the friendly light shining through the window.

"You will come in for coffee perhaps. My grandmother is making it now."

"Your grandmother? Is she in there?" the stranger asked.

"Why not? It's getting colder by the minute. Please come in before I freeze."

"I will come," said the stranger, "and I thank you."

"And you?" Alouette turned to the Northern Traveler.

"No, my work finished. I go back my cabin in forest. But I return. Always remember, Northern Traveler keep watch. And when you hear owl hoot three times, and then three times again, you know I come back."

And, as he had done before, the Northern Traveler disappeared toward the North.

"Northward, ever northward," said the stranger. "He is one who never goes astray in the forest."

By this time they were at the door to the kitchen-parlor. "If you will stand still a minute," Alouette said, "I will sweep the snow off your boots. Grandmère is very particular about that."

"Yes, that I know," was the stranger's surprising answer.

"Alouette Robinette, have you gone out of your mind, out there in the lane this time of morning?" It was Grandmère's voice calling from the kitchen-parlor.

"And who are you talking to, if you please?"

"This gentleman, Grandmère. He has come in for coffee."

Alouette opened the door and the stranger stepped into the warm, bright room, fragrant with the aroma of steaming coffee.

"A gentleman . . ." Grandmère had just taken a plate from the cupboard, but when she turned to face Alouette and her guest, the plate crashed to the floor and her face was as white as the driven snow.

She made the sign of the cross, then stared at the stranger as though she were seeing a ghost.

"This is impossible. It can't be," she muttered, and then flung herself into the stranger's outstretched arms.

"*Tante!*" he cried, stroking her hair. "You haven't changed in all these years."

158

"Jacques! My little Jacques! They told us you had gone astray in the winter woods. We did not hear anything else but that. It is almost impossible to survive an ordeal in the forest. How . . . ?"

"But that can come later. I want to talk to Alouette, to thank her for everything she has done to make this reunion possible."

"Alouette, this is your cousin Jacques. You remember him? And what have you been up to?" Grandmère said as an afterthought.

Alouette looked at the handsome man who stood before her.

"Alouette has been up to a great deal, a great deal, as you will learn," he explained.

Alouette thought his eyes had a sad look in them, like one who has had much sorrow. It was no time for sorrowful thoughts though, and Alouette came straight to the point.

"Well, my goodness! Now you and the white-haired Mamselle can be married at last."

At this Cousin Jacques' eyes took on a pleasant twinkle and he gave one of his cousin's spiky pigtails a playful twitch.

"Out of the mouths of babes, eh?"

But Alouette did not hear. She had hastened upstairs to dress for breakfast.

At breakfast, after the excitement of his return had died down, Jacques told them his story. He had indeed taken a wrong turn and gone astray. But the Northern Traveler had found him, more dead than alive, and nursed him back to health in his cabin in the forest.

After he regained his health, he went to Manitoba, where he had prospered. "And, if I do say so myself, I have fared very well," he explained.

"I could not reward the Northern Traveler in any way. He is constantly doing good for others. It was the Northern Traveler who thought I should return to my family . . . it seems in my delirium in the cabin I had told my whole life story.

"But I couldn't bear the thought of the Island without Mamselle, even though the Traveler was making the journey and wanted me to come.

"I had been wearing the cat's eye ring. It was my dearest possession. Then I remembered that it was nearing our little Alouette's birthday, and that she had been named after Mamselle, *my* Alouette. So I bought a golden chain and put the cat's eye ring on it and sent it to Alouette by the Traveler, swearing him to secrecy because I could not face the Island without Mamselle."

"Were you the one who sent the silent old caretaker to the Manor?" Papa asked.

"Yes! I couldn't bear to think of the Manor's being neglected. The Northern Traveler hired the silent one, and through him kept informed as to what was going on at the old house. It was the Northern Traveler who told me of the rescue at sea. Now here I am, back to stay, in my beloved village."

There was a deep silence in the room. Then Grandmère spoke. "Jacques, there is something you must know before you see Mamselle. She will not recognize you. She remembers nothing that occurred before the accident. The doctors have said a shock, even a small one, could restore her memory, but nothing so far has accomplished that."

Jacques was silent now, lost in deep thought. "There must be some way," he said at last. "I shall try to find a way to make her remember."

"Wait, I forgot! The ring!" Alouette muttered and ran up to her room. "The ring," she said, handing it to him. "The cat's eye ring."

"Yes, the cat's eye ring." He slipped it in his breast pocket, over his heart.

"I didn't know who sent it. The Northern Traveler asked me to keep it a secret. Then I saw one like it on Mamselle's finger and I wondered . . ."

Now the whole family was looking at her in amazement.

"Alouette keep a secret? Impossible for that featherhead," said André.

"Pooh!" Alouette tossed her head.

But Cousin Jacques had risen to his feet. "Come with me, Alouette. You started this whole thing. Perhaps we can see it through to a happy ending, eh?"

"Let's go try, Alouette. Suppose we go on snowshoes."

"Don't feel too badly if she doesn't recognize you," Grandmère said again, closing the door, and Cousin Jacques and Alouette set off toward Lonesome Manor.

As they approached the big iron gate Cousin Jacques began to whistle. Loud and clear came the tune:

"Featherhead, Featherhead,
Alouette, Alouette, ah!"

Then, as he stood at the gate, whistling the old folk tune, the door of Lonesome Manor opened.

162

The white-haired Mamselle came running down the path . . . and . . . she was doing an amazing thing. The lady was whistling! The white-haired Mamselle was whistling "Frère Jacques" all the way down to the big iron gate.

Abruptly she stopped whistling and stood looking at Jacques Robinette. Her face was deathly pale.

Alouette felt frightened . . . Mamselle was so silent. Then, as if a great load had been lifted from her mind, she threw herself into Jacques' arms.

"Oh Jacques, you have come back to me at last!"

Jacques held her for a moment, then felt in his pocket. "You see this?" He held up the cat's eye ring, the ring the Northern Traveler had brought to Alouette.

It was no longer on a chain. Jacques laid it in the white-haired Mamselle's hand. "Put it on my finger," he said softly, "as you did before. Now, you have your ring?"

"It has never been off my finger, even when I could not remember where it came from."

"But now you remember?" Jacques asked.

"Oh yes, my father gave us the rings. They had

163

been used in our family for generations as betrothal rings."

"He gave them to us with his blessing," Jacques reminded her as they entered the big hall.

Alouette started to go down the path to the gate. She felt that Jacques and the white-haired Mamselle might wish to be alone together. But it seemed this was not the case.

The front door opened and Jacques called to her. "Come in, Alouette. I want to talk to you for a minute."

"My gracious, what a time to want to talk to *me*," Alouette thought, as she unbuckled her snowshoes and stood them upright beside her cousin's.

"What is it, Jacques?" she asked, as she entered the hall.

"Well, as you know, Mamselle and I were betrothed and the banns were published three times as it is required."

"Yes, I have heard both Maman and Grandmère say this."

"Well, we are still betrothed, and what I want to ask you is this. Do we still have the same good priest here that we had when I went away?"

"Of course, Jacques. He's baptized every little

Robinette born to Maman and Papa, and who knows when he will baptize another one?"

"Hmm . . . well, then, I want to know about the priest because I would like to have him marry us before the *fête* of the little Jesus. I shall go to see him this very day."

"You will indeed!" said a querulous voice. "And who may you be, trying to sweep her ladyship off her feet?"

It was the old Scottish nurse, speaking her mind as usual. "And perhaps you can explain," she said, turning to Mamselle, "why you permit a total stranger to hold you in his arms."

"Nana, this is not a stranger. It is Jacques. Jacques has come home."

"Humbug," growled the old nurse, fumbling for her spectacles. "Humbug," she repeated, and then she found her glasses and put them on. "By the ancient plaid of my ancestors, it is!" Nana cried, peering into his face with her glasses on. "Do you remember him, my lady?"

"I remember everything. Everything came back to me as soon as I heard him whistling at the gate just now."

"Well, the doctors have been saying a shock would do it. I never expected to see it happen. As

165

for myself, I think I'll just sit down for a moment. I've had a bit of a shock myself."

"Mamselle?" A small figure dressed in white stood leaning over the railing on the stair landing.

"Oh, Maria darling, come down and meet Jacques," Mamselle called.

Maria raced down the red-carpeted stairs. "I was so afraid you'd forget me if you remembered the past again."

"Come here, Maria," said Cousin Jacques seriously, "and you too, Alouette. I have something to tell you that will make you both happy. Mamselle and I are going to be married as soon as the good priest will permit. Then, and what do you think of this, Maria? We are going to take out adoption papers at once. Mamselle will be Maman. I will be Papa. You will be a real Robinette then, and goodness knows that's having a family, eh?"

"The cradle is never empty," Alouette said, laughing. "That's the Robinettes for you."

Then she remembered something. "Tell me," she said, tugging at her cousin's coat, "tell me this. You and Mamselle have the cat's eye rings that are exactly alike, only the one the Northern Traveler gave me has a name in it and Mamselle's ring does not have a name in it. Why is that?"

166

"Neither ring has a name in it, Alouette," Jacques said, looking at her with a puzzled expression.

"I have looked at the ring every night since the Northern Traveler brought it from Manitoba. It is there as plain as day. The name is *Mizpah.*"

"Oh, surely," Jacques nodded seriously. "*Mizpah* is engraved in both rings, but it is not a name."

"What then?"

"It is an ancient word and it means—" Cousin Jacques looked deeply into Mamselle's blue eyes now—"it means," he said softly, "The Lord watch between me and thee while we are absent one from another."

CHAPTER 12

Joyeux Noël

COUSIN JACQUES carried out his word to the letter. That very same day he went to the good priest. The priest remembered very well that the wedding banns of the white-haired Mamselle and Jacques, set down in the archives of the church as Alouette McPherson and Jacques Robinette, had been published six years ago. Everything had been done with the approval of the Church. There was nothing to prevent his performing the happy marriage at once.

After a short wedding trip to Montreal, the newlyweds were back home again.

Lonesome Manor had dropped its mantle of sadness. Now it had taken its rightful place as a home,

169

lived in and loved. Lights twinkled from its windows at dusk as cheerfully as the lamplight of the neighboring farmhouses.

Alouette tried very hard to call her new cousin by her real name, Alouette, but she always ended by calling her Mamselle.

"Why is it?" she asked Grandmère one day shortly after the wedding, as the old lady sat at her spinning wheel, "why is it that no one can remember to call the white-haired Mamselle by her real name?"

Grandmère looked over her spectacles and smiled. "People do not change overnight, my little one. She has always been known hereabouts by that name and she always will be. The only one who refers to her otherwise is her husband. Jacques sometimes calls her 'Featherhead' in fun."

Now another excitement hung in the air . . . the excitement of Christmas, the birthday of the little Jesus.

The white-haired Mamselle had insisted that the entire Robinette family come to the Manor for dinner on Christmas Day. "Impossible," Maman had said. "There are too many of us."

"Poof!" said Mamselle, as she and Maman sat

over afternoon tea at the farmhouse. "And poof again. What is Christmas without a family?"

"On one condition we will come," Maman said, setting down her teacup firmly, "on one condition only. Grandmère and I will roast two fat geese and bring them to the Manor piping hot."

Mamselle nodded. "All right, if you insist."

So now at last it was the day before Christmas. The farmhouse was in its usual Christmas uproar. Children seemed to be underfoot everywhere. Chichi and the twins had to be watched every moment. They were scribbling notes to Father Christmas and sending them up the chimney.

"I want a big doll that bends in the middle and says *Maman, Papa, Grandmère,* and *Alouette,"* Chichi informed her sister.

"And where would you find such a doll as that?"

"Father Christmas will find it," Chichi said firmly.

"Alouette, you'll have to go to Ste. Famille for a packet of sage." Maman stood beside the kitchen table, her arms white with flour. "I want to stuff the geese tonight, so I can start them early in the morning. You can't stuff a goose properly without sage. André will keep an eye on the small ones while you are gone."

"I have to do everything," André grumbled.

"You went to the store this morning," his sister reminded him and, warmly bundled in her heavy coat and hood with the pompons, she mounted the wooden seat of the big sledge and went whistling gaily down the road.

Gossip Madame Durand, at her window as usual, watched with curious eyes. "Look at that one," she said to her husband. "Where could she be going this late in the afternoon? There she goes, lickety-split, whistling as usual. I always say a whistling girl and a crowing hen . . ."

But Madame got no further. Her husband rose from his chair. "Silence, woman!" he roared. The patient spouse of the village gossip had reached the limit of his endurance.

But Alouette, unaware of the tempest in a teapot she had created, continued to whistle as the old sledge went bumping over the road.

Everything spoke of Christmas in the narrow streets of Ste. Famille. Villagers hurried along through the whirling snowflakes, anxious to be home to a good hot supper and then to attend the services at the lovely little country church.

Alouette put the red blanket over Herbert, and went into the store of Henri Tremblay.

172

"Maman sent me for a packet of sage," she said when Henri came forward to wait on her.

"Tell me," he said after he had handed her the sage, "is it true that you are dining at the Manor tomorrow night?"

Alouette nodded, "Yes."

"Well then, why is your mother roasting a goose?"

Alouette laughed at the storekeeper's interest. "Because Maman has roasted a goose every Christmas since she's been married, I guess. She just couldn't think of not doing it."

"She is taking the goose to the Manor then?"

"Geese it has to be," Alouette said. "There are too many of us for just one goose."

Henri nodded. "This will be of interest to the Snow Man. He will be coming in soon to hear the news."

"Such a business," Alouette said aloud to Herbert as she removed his blanket and climbed in the sleigh. "Maman cannot even roast a goose without someone talking about it. It's nice though, Herbert, when people take a friendly interest, eh?"

Now she was out of the village and back on the white road, going lickety-split toward home.

"How pleasant to see the lights in the old Manor

House," she thought. "I have to pinch myself to believe it."

She arrived home just in time to unhitch Herbert and feed him before the family sat down for supper.

Now it was truly Christmas Eve . . . beautiful as it is beautiful only in French Canada. The snow storm had ceased and a radiant, starlit sky shone on the white world.

It was time to go to the white church. Herbert and the sledge were once again waiting in the lane. All the Robinettes, even Baby, were bundled to their noses, covered with blankets and bearskin robes, warm charcoal burners at their feet.

As they drove, they saw farmers and their families coming from every direction, swinging lanterns as they made their way to the church.

"This is the Christmas country," Alouette thought, as she watched the lanterns throwing their orange-colored light on the snow.

And when they reached the church it was perfumed with the fragrance of the pine woods. Candlelight flickered over the Holy Family in the *crèche,* and the boughs of evergreens and firs.

It was a beautiful and solemn service, and when it was over, the stars were still shining. One star

seemed brighter to Alouette. She spoke to Grandmère, who was sitting beside her in the sledge.

"That star seems to be guiding us home," she
said.

"Yes, it is leading us on our way, telling us to
walk with God," Grandmère said.

The star was still there when Alouette looked
through her window after she had blown out her
lamp. The lovely star seemed to lend radiance
to the snow-mantled world. And it stayed there,
shining down on the peaceful farmhouse, long
after she had drifted off to sleep.

"*Joyeux Noël!*" A chorus of voices greeted her
as she came downstairs Christmas morning. They
were all there waiting for her in the little hall.
The kitchen-parlor door was closed. But now, as
Alouette set foot in the hall, Grandpère put his
hand on the door. "Now then, we will see if
Father Christmas came last night, eh?" he said.

He threw open the door then, and the children
stood looking into the room with round eyes.

"The Christmas tree is wonderful," Alouette
gasped. "It seems every year our Christmas trees
get more beautiful."

The tree was so tall it reached the ceiling. Green
and sparkling it was standing between the two

175

front windows as the snow storm whirled outside, tapping at the windowpanes and drifting into fence-corners.

Gilded walnuts and strings of popcorn, colored paper chains, and ropes of bright cranberries were festooned over the tree, decorating it in true farm fashion.

A hundred bright little candles and sparkling artificial snow were the only things that had not been made by loving hands at home.

Underneath the tree were presents for all. There were new skates for all except Baby, who got a rattle tinkling with silver bells, mittens, sweaters and woolen hose, drums and horns for the twins, a bright new sled and a new winter jacket from the Hudson Bay trading post for André. For Alouette there were a new dress, two new pinafores and, best of all, a little brown fur muff that matched the collar on her new red coat.

Chichi found a dress and pinafore with her name on them, but had eyes only for the big doll that said *Maman* when you bent her in the middle. The little girl did not seem to mind that Father Christmas had neglected to make the doll say *Papa, Grandmère,* and *Alouette.*

There were a very handsome new blanket of

Scotch plaid for Herbert, a new collar for Armand, and red ribbon bows for Minou and the kittens. Christmas was everywhere in the big comfortable room.

"This is a day to make all the good saints happy," Alouette sighed blissfully. "And to think it is just beginning."

"Maman says we can expect to see another Christmas tree tonight in the big hall at the Manor. Cousin Jacques told her there would be surprises there, too," André said. "But I don't see how it can be better than this one."

Now while all this excitement was going on it was not an easy thing to keep the children away from the stove where two fine fat geese were roasting for the dinner at the Manor. But somehow Maman managed to shoo them away . . . all but Alouette, who flitted about, bustling with responsibility.

Dinner was to be at four, and now the baskets were packed with freshly baked bread, homemade cheese, blueberry jam, rolls and sweet butter. Most important of all were the plump roasted geese, filling the air with rich fragrance as they were carried out piping hot in their roasting pans, and packed in the big sledge.

Alouette dressed in her Sunday best, which now included the fur muff as well as the little round hat. She was going on snowshoes, as was André. The rest of the family went a little ahead of them, snugly tucked into the big sledge, with Herbert's single bell ringing loudly on the frosty air.

Alouette looked at the village in the distance. "Ste. Famille looks like a toy village under a Christmas tree," she said as she and André trudged along on snowshoes.

"How can that be?" asked the literal André.

"Oh, all sparkly and shining . . ." but she interrupted herself. "Look . . . look at the Manor, André, look at it," she gasped as they reached the big iron gates.

It was beginning to get dark, for night falls early in the wintertime in Canada.

"Every window has a holly wreath and a lighted candle in it. Did you ever see anything so beautiful?"

There had been a thaw earlier in the day, but now it had grown colder and was snowing again. Every turret and tower on the old Manor was gleaming with icicles behind a softly falling veil of snow.

"An enchanted castle," Alouette breathed as

they reached the steps to the Manor and stood their snowshoes upright in the drift.

Maria's fair head popped out the door as they went up the steps. "Oh, Alouette, guess what? I got snowshoes for Christmas. Will you teach me how to walk on them?"

"Teach you to walk on snowshoes? My goodness, I thought everyone knew how to do that. Of course I'll teach you."

They had reached the veranda now and as Alouette stood in the doorway, she turned to Maria and said, "It really is a fairy castle, inside and out."

"And you are the good fairy who made it that way," Maria said as she closed the door behind Alouette and André. "Let me take your things," she said politely.

Alouette handed over her coat and hat, and even forgot for the moment to show Maria the little fur muff.

The great hall was decorated with fragrant ropes of evergreens and holly. The grandfather clock on the landing peered through a holly wreath, and the secret panel was festooned with sweet-smelling branches of fir. A Yule log was blazing in the fireplace, and beside it stood the Christmas tree.

"It is a lovely tree," Alouette said, "and you

know what? It is trimmed just like ours with cranberries and popcorn and colored paper chains. I am glad it is not trimmed with store-bought things. This way is better."

"Of course it is better," said the white-haired Mamselle. "Remember always the farmer's way is a good way of doing things, doing things with our own hands."

The subject changed abruptly. "What smells so good?" Maria asked, crinkling her nose at the delicious aroma coming from the kitchen.

"The geese are burning up, I guess," Chichi volunteered.

"Chichi, hush, it is wicked to be naughty on the *fête* of the little Jesus," Alouette reminded her.

"Let's see if the geese are burned up," Cousin Jacques said, and threw open the double doors and there stood the long table set with delicate china and silver and glass. The geese, one at each end of the table, occupied the places of honor, but there were venison too, and partridges, and the traditional boar's head, gaily decked with a red apple in its mouth.

"Everything your heart could wish for," Alouette said, as they all filed in and took their places at the table.

Grandpère, being the head of the family, asked a blessing while they all bowed their heads reverently. But after that there was such a chatter that, as Maman said later, it sounded like a nest of squirrels.

Finally the pudding was brought in, flaming and surrounded by holly. And after that the feast was over.

Beneath the Christmas tree, Cousin Jacques began calling out names written on mysterious packages. For André, skis; for Grandmère and Maman, each a fine fur cape; for Chichi, a doll house completely furnished; hobby horses for the twins, as well as a soft white coat and hood for Baby, who was still too small to know what Christmas meant. Grandpère and Papa were both given a fine Hudson's Bay coat, and Nana got a violet-colored wool coat and a silk dress to match.

"No more solemn black for you," Cousin Jacques warned, "and no more sour faces, mind you." And he gave the old nurse a hug when she hobbled over to receive her gift.

"Now we'll get down to the rest of the Manor house family," Cousin Jacques said, and he handed the white-haired Mamselle a white velvet box.

"Oh it's the most gorgeous thing I ever saw,"

Mamselle gasped, and held up a necklace of sparkling green stones that matched the stones in the cat's eye ring.

"It is an antique necklace," Jacques said. "I bought it in Montreal. It just seemed to belong with your ring." He looked proudly at Mamselle's left hand where the cat's eye ring now shared the third finger with a gold wedding band.

"And for Maria, then, what did Father Christmas leave for her?" He scratched his head. "Oh, yes, in Montreal that same day I saw . . ." and he handed her a blue velvet box and a tiny white one.

"Bracelets . . . blue enamel, and a ring with a little diamond. How beautiful" And Maria put the lovely bracelets on, one on each arm, and the small diamond ring on her finger.

"And another thing," said Cousin Jacques, "that day in Montreal we filed adoption papers for you, my little one. It won't be long now until you will be Maria Robinette. You will have a maman and a papa and lots of cousins. You will like that, eh?"

Maria flung herself against him and hugged him at the prospect of the happiness ahead.

"And now then we have only the silent one," Cousin Jacques said, and as the old man slipped forward he presented him with a fine warm suit and winter coat. Then the strangest thing of all happened.

"Thank you," said the silent one, in as loud and clear a speech as anyone could wish for.

"My word!" Alouette gasped. "Why haven't you ever talked to us before?"

"Didn't have anything to say," said the silent one and he strode from the room without another word.

Now the farm family were presenting their gifts. Practical and useful gifts they were, and made with loving hearts and busy hands.

"Well, I guess that just about finishes, eh?"

Cousin Jacques looked from one face to another. All were smiling . . . all but Alouette.

Her cousin looked at her searchingly. "Don't tell me Father Christmas forgot you," he said, scratching his nose meditatingly.

Alouette, fighting back the tears, could only nod.

"Well, come with me then at once."

Alouette put on her hat and coat. "Where are we going?"

"We could be going to the North Pole."

But, as it turned out, they ended up at the stable.

The door slid open and there was a shower of sleigh bells.

Alouette's eyes were as large as saucers, for out came a small black pony. She was pulling a small and shining new red sleigh.

"Try it for size, my little one."

"Me?" In a daze Alouette got into the soft leather seat.

"Let her go around to the garden a little and see how it works," Cousin Jacques commanded.

Alouette drove around in a circle and returned. "This little sleigh glides like a bird. It doesn't go bumpity-bump at all."

She got out and laid her face against the black pony's soft white nose. "She has a little star on her head. She is for Maria, perhaps?"

"Maria? What a thought. Maria can share Colette. It is for you . . . a small reward for all the happiness you have brought us," he said quietly.

Alouette laid her cheek against the pony's nose. "I love her, the little Star."

"So you've named her Star, eh? Just the right name for her."

"Yes, Star, but . . . but . . ." and much to her cousin's surprise Alouette burst into tears.

"Here, no crying on Christmas or we'll have to

send the little Star back. Whatever is the matter with you, Alouette Robinette?"

"It is . . . it is . . . about Herbert," she explained, still sniffing and fumbling in her coat pocket for her handkerchief.

"Oh here, use mine." Alouette accepted the proffered handkerchief gratefully.

"Now what is this about Herbert?"

"Well, I can't bear to have him hauling that old sledge around while I drive a fine new sleigh. Herbert never had a decent sleigh."

"He didn't, eh?" Cousin Jacques strode into the stable. "What do you think of this then?"

And through the stable came Herbert, drawing a shiny black sleigh and wearing a new harness with jingling bells.

"How handsome he looks. I never saw a sleigh with three seats." Alouette went over and gave Herbert a big hug.

"It takes three seats when the Robinettes go sleighing. Are you happy now?"

"The happiest girl in the world," Alouette replied.

"Oh, before you get in, here is a little something else that belongs to you." He opened a small velvet box, and winking up at her was the golden chain that the Northern Traveler had given her that snowy evening by the gate. Only this time, there was no cat's eye ring on the chain, but a small golden locket set with turquoise and pearls.

"Open it," Cousin Jacques commanded, and when she did, she found two tiny pictures smiling at her. They were pictures of Cousin Jacques and the white-haired Mamselle.

"Oh, thank you." And Alouette started to cry again.

"Hop in the little sleigh, and drive around to the veranda. I'll follow with Herbert. And stop that crying," Cousin Jacques said kindly, "or everybody will think you don't want the little Star."

"Does everybody know about Star and the red sleigh?"

"Of course everyone has known, that is everyone but Chichi."

"Well, I would have known if Chichi did. *That* one can't keep a secret."

"Start up now, Alouette. They are all waiting on the veranda, ready to go home."

And as the little sleigh went gliding and jingling up to the Manor house, they were all waiting for her outside.

"You lead off with Chichi and André," Cousin

Jacques told Alouette, "then the rest will follow with Herbert and the new sleigh."

So, after goodby's and thank you's were said, Alouette gave Star her first command. "Whoa!" she said, and as the little pony obeyed, André lifted Chichi in and sat down beside her.

"*Joyeux Noël,*" everyone cried.

"Goodby, goodby," cried the white-haired Mamselle, as she and Maria and Jacques stood waving.

"Remember, Alouette, we owe all our happiness to you."

Alouette waved back and the little Star set off. With jingling harness, the little red sleigh went gliding down the long white road. Behind them came Herbert, proudly drawing his own jingling sleigh containing the rest of the family, and piled high with gifts and the forgotten showshoes.

"There is something in your coat pocket," Chichi said. "It's a secret. I saw Mamselle put it there."

Alouette put her mittened hand in her pocket and found the little musical clock. "Secret, eh?" she said laughing. "You'll never know what a secret this little clock really kept."

Then she turned to André. "It is a wonderful

187

thing that the beautiful Manor house will never again be called Lonesome Manor."

"Yes, and do you know who is responsible for all these doings?"

Alouette did not reply. She was listening to the jingle of Star's sleigh bells as they glided over the long white road that led to the farmhouse.

"I will tell you who is responsible," André insisted.

"Tell away, then."

André began to sing:

> "Featherhead, Featherhead,
> Alouette, Alouette, ah!"

And, for the first time, Alouette did not say "Pooh!"